FRANKENSTEIN'S BRIDE

FRANKENSTEIN'S BRIDE

———————— • ————————

HILARY BAILEY

———————— • ————————

SIMON & SCHUSTER

LONDON · SYDNEY · NEW YORK · TOKYO · SINGAPORE · TORONTO

First published in Great Britain
by Simon & Schuster Ltd, 1995
A Paramount Communications Company

Simon & Schuster Ltd
West Garden Place
Kendal Street
London W2 2AQ

Simon & Schuster of Australia Pty Ltd
Sydney

A CIP catalogue record for this book is
available from the British Library

ISBN 0–671–71917–3

Printed and bound in Great Britain by
Butler & Tanner Ltd, Frome and London

'YOU MUST CREATE A FEMALE FOR ME . . .'

'As I proceeded in my labour it became every day more horrible and irksome to me.

'Three years before I had created a fiend whose unparalleled barbarity had desolated my heart and filled it forever with bitterest remorse. I was now about to form another being of whose disposition I was alike ignorant; she might become ten thousand times more malignant than her mate and delight, for its own sake, in murder and wretchedness.

'I thought, with a sensation of madness, of creating another like to him and, trembling with passion, tore to pieces the thing on which I was engaged.'

Frankenstein by Mary Shelly 1818

To Joshua Alwyne Compton,
Marquis of Northampton,
President of the Royal Society, London

August 31st, 1846
Kittering Hall, Nottingham

My Lord,

You will recall, I believe, our meeting at the house of my wife's kinsman Mr Flint. After dinner you made mention of the curious old story of the death of Victor Frankenstein over twenty years ago now, and of the rumours that have since circulated round his name.

Perhaps you will recall my confiding privately to you later that evening that I had been a friend of Mr Frankenstein, had been a witness and sometimes a participant in the events surrounding his death. I added that I had a full account, made from notes concerning the affair kept daily around the turn of the year 1825 – that in my possession I had also Mr

Frankenstein's scientific notes and diagrams made over many years – and also his own account of his life and the events leading up to his death. I believe I told you that my ownership of these papers had made, and was making me increasingly, uneasy. I think I may say that this information caused you much astonishment. You were good enough to suggest that if I would send you my account of the life – and death – of Mr Frankenstein, as well as papers of his I have in my possession, you would be content to read the documents and appraise them, volunteering to give me some idea of what, in your opinion, I should do with the material.

I now gladly send you these papers, happy to be able to share the burden of them with a man of such reputation as your own. I fear the contents may shock you gravely, although I venture to guess they will also interest you greatly. I give you my assurance that all you read is true to the best of my belief.

I remain, thanking you for your goodness in undertaking the task of reading this account, your obedient servant. My Lord,

Jonathan Goodall

ONE

The tale I have to tell, my Lord, which for twenty years or more I have kept to myself, is a strange and terrifying one. There are those who might say it would be better to leave the story forever untold. Yet, as a man reaches a certain age he must, perforce, settle his debts and fulfil his obligations to those who will live after him. I do not believe that in my case this ordering of affairs should stop at my own gates. I believe it is my duty, my debt to the past, to tell the story I have to tell.

So I will relate the history of my friend, the unfortunate Victor Frankenstein, the story of a soul which took itself to perdition, a man who was the author of his own, terrible, downfall. Whether my revelations will bring good or evil in themselves I am unable to predict.

My story begins in November 1825 – but first I will say something of myself as I then was, a young man of not quite thirty years, healthy, not poor, a possessor, I

believe, of a cheerful disposition, the only great grief of
my life having been, up to that point, the death of my
dearly loved mother when I was but fifteen years old.
The remainder of my family, my father and two younger
sisters, Arabella and Anna, resided near Nottingham at
Kittering Hall, in a house which had been owned by
our family for more than a hundred years. In that
neighbourhood lived also many friends and kinsfolk.
Our family believed we had been in the neighbourhood,
farming our land since the Domesday Book. What family
does not? But there are records to prove that, if we had
not been there quite since the first William's time, the
Goodalls had been for long enough as honest a family as
any in the county, being careful landlords, maintaining
the common land, showing justice to their tenants and in
the years just preceding the time of which I write, having
lowered their rents during the bad years following the
war against Napoleon. But I digress. Suffice it to say
the family did its duty and over the years produced its
own share of honest doctors, lawyers, magistrates and
the like.

In the later years of my grandfather's life, though,
came a change in the family fortunes – not, as these
words normally mean for the worse but for the better.
Grandfather discovered coal on our land, whereupon
fields which had formerly produced a modest income
through tilling and grazing became the source of considerable profit to us. To cut the story short, then, that
black crop from our fields made of me a young man with
no need to earn my bread by the sweat of my brow or the
scratch of my pen. I was thus able to pursue a course
of study without care. It was, as it turned out, through

these studies that the connection between myself and Victor Frankenstein arose.

Having almost enjoyed my schooldays, which is, I believe, as much as any man can honestly say, I rejoiced in my years at Oxford. In addition to the normal pursuits of a man in his university years such as friendships, suppers, rowing, horseplay and disturbing the peace of the worthy, I took greatly to the study of languages, not for themselves alone but for what they indicate about the lives of men and the operations of the many different societies in which they live. So I graduated from Oxford not merely skilled in the arts of port and claret – and love, which I took lightly, though, I hope, leaving neither myself nor my beloved of the time any worse off than either of us had been before – but also as something of a scholar in philology.

In the beginning was the Word, says St John the Divine. The study of language is the study of man, for it is language which distinguishes man from the beast, language alone which allows us to convey higher thoughts, scientific, religious or poetic. Through the study of languages and their origins we may learn much of ourselves. King James I, it is said, suffered a baby to be put in a pit for seven years, without seeing any human being during all that time, on the grounds that when pulled up the child might speak Latin!

I came to London to work on my dictionary of Aramaic, the very tongue in which Our Lord spoke. My friend David Hathaway, a printer and publisher, has since published this work – though at the time of which I speak he was still waiting for me to complete it.

One evening I attempted to explain my theories of

languages to my landlady Cordelia Downey. She, I am afraid, laughed at me. 'Why,' she exclaimed, looking up, I believe from the mending of her little daughter's stockings, and fixing me with her large, bright, blue eyes, 'language is a simple thing, we learn it as babies, babbling and mumbling as we attempt to copy the speech of our elders. And that,' said she, 'Mr Goodall, is that.'

'Then why are there so many tongues?' I questioned. 'Why do we not all, from here to China, use the same language? What of that *speaking with tongues* when, as the Bible tells us, each man in the crowd at Jerusalem to celebrate Pentecost, wherever he came from and whatever tongue he spoke, could understand the other? What of oracular speech, what of speech when we dream – whence come those voices when the conscious mind is not in control?'

Well, I regret to say that Mrs Downey offered no answer to these questions. Instead she gave a puzzled frown, followed by a dismissive noise – I will not call it a snort – and then turned to cutting out a small dress for her daughter. Women in general have little taste for the speculative, preferring the here and now of things. Yet it was those studies of mine, however arcane they may have appeared to Mrs Downey, which led to my part in the sad and horrifying tale of Victor Frankenstein and, I believe, changed my view of life completely.

However, at the time when my story begins I was a contented man, the times we lived in forced no great efforts on us. The war with France was over; the country at peace.

As I look back, to use an image drawn from science,

I see my younger self as unshaped and undefined, a mass of gases, so to speak, made up of my own natural qualities and of my circumstances in life, waiting only for the catalyst which would turn those gases into solid form – my later self. To think that these changes came through the study of philology! For that was the reason why, to take you to the heart of the tale, that on that November afternoon of which I spoke earlier I found myself walking through rapidly swelling river fog, at dusk, beside the Thames, looking longingly but with little hope for a conveyance I could hire to take me back to my lodgings in Gray's Inn Road.

I had arrived by the riverside on foot to visit my friend Dr Victor Frankenstein at his house in Cheyne Walk. I regretted having to make my way home by the same means, for the fog thickened, it grew ever darker and I was alone.

There was not a soul about as I trod the road which lies beyond the northern bank of London's great river. Missing the warmth and hospitality of Victor and Elizabeth Frankenstein's house, I hurried on, not altogether happy about the prospect of a dark and foggy walk through the suburbs of London. The fields, manufactories and market gardens beside the road on which I was travelling were deserted at that season and hour. All were places where a footpad or some other assailant could lurk undetected – and I had no stick or cudgel with me.

It was at this point that, looking down towards the strand, I spotted, by the light of a flaming torch which had been set up on a small wharf below the road, a massive and extraordinary figure. He stood on a small stone quay built out a little distance into the river. On this tiny wharf, only about fifteen feet wide and twenty across, men were unloading large crates and some barrels from a barge which had come from upriver. In astonishment I gazed at this monstrous figure, almost six-and-a-half feet tall, I judged, and correspondingly massive, clad in what seemed like a long, ragged black coat with flapping sleeves. He was bare-headed, and dark, flowing locks hung to his shoulders. As the barge slipped and slopped at anchorage this man I noted with such awe and disbelief was bending into the vessel, seizing wooden boxes from within, then, with enormously powerful movements, half-throwing them on to the jetty. The weight of the boxes to an ordinary man could be judged by the efforts his companions were making with the others. Where they strained, the other threw them about like so many children's bricks.

There came a cry, as the men hurled one on to a pile on the jetty, as if the crate had struck, or almost struck, another man. Yet, as if in a frenzy to get done, he continued to haul them out, not acknowledging the protest. Then came another cry. The ogre (for so he seemed), then clambered in an ungainly way into the barge, apparently dragging a crippled leg behind him, and went on unloading from inside the vessel. I watched him stagger a little as the water moved the barge, then raise a cask above his head and almost hurl it into the arms of another man, who reeled and nearly lost his footing. Someone, to provide more illumination, set light to a pile of wood and tarred rope on the jetty. Just as the resultant stench struck me, the light caught this vast creature, flickered away with the wind, then caught him again, revealing him more clearly. The face was heavy-browed, heavy-jawed and seemed twisted somehow, as if malformed at birth. It was a face such as one sees sometimes on those unfortunate enough to have come into the world feeble-minded. I could not see his eyes. They were hidden under jutting brows. His shoulder-length black hair blew about in the wind. I noted his feet were bare – cruel in such weather.

As he stood on that swaying deck I thought of some old figure from mythology, half-brute, half-human. So seized was I by this extraordinary spectacle I forgot for a moment my predicament, alone in freezing fog and darkness, yet as it came back to me, to my horror, the creature threw back his head and gave a great howl, a howl of agony. I do not know how to describe this sound. It was not the cry of a wolf or other beast but the cry of a man, as if in unbearable pain. And as he howled he pointed an arm in a flapping sleeve, in my direction. I froze – but no – he had not seen me, found some mad prejudice against me. He was pointing beyond me, and a little to my right, up the strand, across the road in the direction of the houses of Cheyne Walk, the direction whence I had just come.

The bargee, at the head of his barge while the off-loading proceeded, did not hesitate. He leapt instantly from his position, crossed the body of his vessel and brought up his arm and crashed some heavy object, a bludgeon or a piece of wood across the side of the head of the pointing figure. Then, shouting something I could not properly hear, he did the same thing again, with all his force. In the face of the blows which would have toppled a normal man, this ogre dropped his pointing arm and threw it round his head, to ward them off - and went back to his work again.

And I, suddenly more afraid of all this than I was of my lonely walk, hurried away, dreading footpads less than something so terrifying, so pathetic and, I sensed, so contrary both to Nature and civilisation. Yet I told myself, walking the ruts of the road from Chelsea, this was surely only a sad example of an idiot, a poor creature lacking in his wits, distorted in body, face and mind; no doubt hideously exploited for his strength by his fellow man. He would be paid little and beaten when he would not work. I pitied him and pondered why God, in his wisdom, had seen fit to make so many of his creatures fall so short of the Divine. Came the heretical thought that perhaps our world is not controlled by God but is an arena for the eternally waged battle between God and his opponent. Had that creature on the strand been created at some time or in some place where the Devil reigned? Men have been burned at the stake for saying aloud what I then thought.

I did not know then that man was not made either by God or the Devil, but by a far more terrible creator – another man.

I sped my steps along the river, through the wastes of Pimlico and eventually to the Strand, where the increasing light from windows and busier streets encouraged me. I slowed my pace and, much in need of warmth and company, I broke my journey at the Voyagers' Club in Covent Garden, where I enjoyed, by an encouraging fire, an hour's respite with friends of a like turn of mind, speaking of fossils with Knight, and the natural roots of our language with Smith. I mentioned to no one the sight I had just seen. It seemed at the time to be one of those scenes one witnesses, a scene that produces a little, momentary curiosity and then is done, forgotten.

Some days later the grim story I must now relate began in earnest, but forgive me if I go back from that figure on the waterfront at Chelsea to speak of the previous summer, when the world was still young and I first met my friend Victor Frankenstein.

Two

I and Victor met on a cricket field! Though Swiss and having passed most of his life in that country or in others more remote, Victor, having arrived with his wife in this country only a few years earlier, was promptly introduced to the game by Hugo Feltham, who had been a fellow student at the University of Ingolstadt in Germany. Hugo had later come on to Oxford, which is where we two had met and become friends. Thus it came about that, as soon as I arrived at Hugo's home, Old Hall, at Longtree in Kent, I was directed by his mother, on Hugo's instructions, to the village green. Her message was that the annual cricket match between Upper and Lower Longtree, always hotly contested, was now taking place. Hugo, she told me, urgently required my services as a batsman, one of the team having been enticed away by the other side, yet another having absconded from the village with another man's wife.

Leaving my horse at the house I walked through the

pleasant grounds of Old Hall. A small gate in the wall took me through the fields of the home farm, where corn was already tall under the July sun. I passed the church and went down the village street, a matter of a draper's forge and two inns, and arrived at the village green, where stood a mighty oak of the kind always described as having sheltered King Charles I when in flight from his enemies; and beyond that, what a heart-lifting sight lay ahead of me! Spread out over the greensward in the sunshine were thirteen men, some in white trousers and shirts, others in their day-to-day moleskins, with flannel shirtsleeves rolled up. Even as I stood beneath the massive oak, watching, I saw a burly fellow in brown trousers with a white shirt open at the throat swing his bat and send the ball flying high in the air, away from where I stood and into a clump of trees on the other side of the green. I heard Hugo's enthusiastic voice – 'Well played, Simcox.'

Hugo himself lay extended on the grass in a cluster of spectators and players, which included some ladies in pale dresses and straw hats. Spotting me as I walked towards them, Hugo leapt to his feet and came towards me, arms extended, beaming and pushing his long fair hair from his face in the way I so well remembered. 'Jonathan!' he cried. 'Welcome, thrice welcome, my dear fellow.'

'Your mother informs me that you need me,' I responded.

'We do indeed, my dear,' he told me, 'for we're almost out and fifty runs behind. Only three men to go. Those ruffians of Lower Longtree have seduced away our blacksmith, who is to marry the daughter of the captain of their team. We lost a second player in another affair of the heart, he and his inamorata having left for London on Tuesday. Love has no scruples, as we know. At the wicket now is one of our footmen, a sturdy fellow in his father's trousers, which he wears for luck, and our local inn-keeper, who, you will see, shows all the signs of having over-imbibed his own wares. He describes himself as feeling as if struck by a cricket ball, which he shortly will be – Ah!' he exclaimed as the other team cried out, 'There! He's lost his wicket. Now it's up to you, Jonathan. We have only you and my good friend Victor now between us and defeat. Let us demand a pause of a few minutes while I take you to meet him.' And Hugo, signalling to the captain of the other side, led me across to the group on the grass.

I loved Hugo, an excellent friend and a truly happy man. He had little to make him unhappy, coming, as he did, from a good, sound family, heir to a prosperous estate and enjoying the love of his family and his charming wife Lucy, mother of two healthy boys. Yet, even as I followed him across the grass I reflected that one man, given the best of circumstances, can still find misery, even ruin if he so wishes, while another can often wring contentment from disaster. We now came up to Hugo's party, where his wife sat on a stool, her boys at her feet; his father was ensconced in dignity on a chair placed there specially for him. After I had greeted them, Hugo said, 'Now meet my friend Victor Frankenstein and his wife Elizabeth, whom we all love.'

Thus, for the first time, I encountered Victor Frankenstein. His wife first – a delightfully dressed, very pretty blonde woman, seated on a stool, with a little boy of about two, very like her, on her lap. Then – Victor, who stood to greet me. He was a tall, well-knit man, with dark brown hair, an oval face tanned by the sun and large brown eyes of the most alert, sympathetic kind. He smiled, showing white, even teeth and took my hand in a firm grasp. At first sight he was a man the gods had smiled on, a man with all the virtues. Later, I found him a little serious, a little melancholy, lacking the lightness and humour so prized by Englishmen, but none the worse for that.

Yet on that sunny day, as Hugo pushed me forward on to the pitch, thrusting a bat in my hand, I saw no traces of that fundamental gravity of Victor's as he smiled and said, 'Come on then. It is all for you to do now.' Then he added, 'Let us talk later – I have been abroad for a good many years, studying languages. Hugo tells me you have interests of that kind.' And, 'I look forward to it,' said I as we parted and I advanced to the wicket.

There are those, not a few, who grow weary at accounts of cricket matches, fencing bouts and the hedge-by-hedge, gate-by-gate tales of the last hunt, so I will abridge my story of our narrow defeat at the hands of Lower Longtree. Suffice it to say that a twisting ball from the hands of the defaulting blacksmith had Simcox the footman out, so I was joined on the field by Victor Frankenstein. As we had walked over to meet him Hugo had explained he put him in late, so as not to offend local susceptibilities, not wishing it to appear he had imported a talented visitor, and a foreigner to boot, to win the match. But I had been sceptical about the gifts of Frankenstein, since I knew he had not learned the game in youth. He proved to be one of those individuals gifted with a natural coordination of hand and eye, capable of shining at any game after very little practice. He had a tall, agile body, not apparently muscular, but stringy and wiry and was soon driving the ball all over the village green. Thus as the sun went down and the shadow of the old oak lengthened and the ladies donned mantles and shawls against the slight chill in the air, we contrived to turn our useful alliance into a pleasant few runs. When I was caught out by the treacherous blacksmith we left the field, defeated but not humiliated.

I shall not easily forget that afternoon, the pleasure of the game, the peace of an English village at play in summer. The cheerful day went on with a barrel of beer produced for the teams and spectators, lemonade for the ladies and children. We gentry soon retired, leaving the villagers to their own celebrations, and returned to Old Hall for a good dinner, with much laughter and conversation.

After dinner, as we sat in the drawing-room with the doors open on to the terrace, the pretty Elizabeth Frankenstein delighted us with some charming songs, Lucy Feltham moved us much with her singing of *The Ash Grove* and we gentlemen rent the ether with some lusty choruses from *The Beggar's Opera*. The guests departed, the household went to bed, but Victor and I repaired to the library where we talked over our wine into the next morning. We spoke of science and our common interest in philology. He himself had spent seven years touring among the Indian tribes of America and attempting to put together a dictionary of their various tongues. Then he had met his wife in Boston and come to settle in England.

I find it hard now, so many years later, to sum up exactly the quality of Victor's mind and conversation. Such things are hard to express. His intelligence was lively as quicksilver, his memory prodigious, yet employed to make connections between one subject and another, constructively, not a mere exercise in the recollection of facts. He expressed himself attractively, his voice low and pleasant and his choice of words and phrases felicitous. When I retired to bed later that night, or rather in the early morning, my mind was buzzing with ideas, all inspired by Victor. What changes, what advances could man not make if only we applied sufficiently our intellect and will? 'Bliss was it in that dawn to be alive, But to be young was very heaven.' Bliss indeed. What a day it had been, I thought, as I fell asleep – carefree and full of all the joys man is heir to: enjoyment of the open air, song, laughter and thought. Yet it was that day of happiness which led me on to others, some of the most gloomy and frightful days of my life.

My poor Victor – it is hard not to believe it was his very virtues which brought about his ruin. He had such energy, such restless curiosity, such a questioning spirit – qualities which may bring greatness to a man and benefits of many kinds to others but which in his case brought him to destruction. Victor was imbued with that feeling of man as his own god, man as capable of constructing his own fate, becoming master of all knowledge or reorganising society according to his own principles and beliefs. This was one of the legacies of the thinking of a previous century, which in effect threw first France, then all Europe, into turmoil. Not

for Victor the common mistakes of youth – riding hell
for leather over the country, breaking his horse's neck
(or his own), spending wildly, falling into the hands of
money-lenders, folly over women, ending in disgrace or
exile. No – Victor's vices had been virtues stood on their
head. In the name of science he challenged the gods and
lost all.

Having gone so late to bed I was late up next morning
(although Victor, I learned, had risen early as usual for
he needed very little sleep). I was on the terrace drinking
some coffee when Hugo joined me, dressed for church.
He asked if I would attend with his family. Victor and
Elizabeth had already said they would go. My agreement
would mean, declared Hugo, that Old Hall would make
as good a display of church-going on Sunday as they had
at cricket the previous day.

How had I enjoyed my conversation with Victor,
Hugo asked. I replied I had rarely enjoyed talking so
much to any man and spoke with great enthusiasm
of Victor's rare intelligence, learning and liveliness of
mind. Victor, I said, appeared to me to be nothing less
than a genius – all the more so as he had told me he came
late to the study of philology, his earlier studies having
been all in the natural sciences. Hugo did not answer
me immediately but after a pause said, rather gravely,
'You are right, Jonathan. When at Ingolstadt Victor
was immersed in studies leagues away from words and
languages.' Then he cheered somewhat and embarked on
an entertaining story of their student days, the substance
of which was that, as a young and extravagant student,
far from home, he had overspent his normal allowance
and this, compounded with the late arrival of money

from home, had prompted his landlady, a ferocious Swiss woman, to become severe with the impecunious English student. In short, she had said if he did not pay the rent immediately, Hugo would find himself in the street. He had therefore rushed to Victor's laboratory and beaten urgently on the door, intending to ask for a loan until his money should arrive. 'And so immersed in his studies was he,' Hugo told me with a smile, 'that though I knew he was inside he did not answer the door to me. I must have hammered on his door in vain for some twenty minutes, calling out his name and my own. I saw his lights, yet he was too engrossed to hear me. That is the nature of the man, that is the nature of his concentration on his work – '

'And you?' I then enquired. 'And your uncharitable landlady?'

'She ejected me,' Hugo smiled. 'I spent an uncomfortable two nights in a graveyard with my baggage around me until my money at last arrived from England, whereupon I secured much better lodgings in the town, where the landlady's soup contained meat, her bread was light and white and her daughter a very pretty girl.'

'You are indeed a man to turn disaster into good cheer,' I said to him affectionately.

'Alas, though,' he responded. 'That was the last time for seven years I saw Victor. For once I was settled in my new lodgings it was soon time for a brief visit to England. When I returned to Ingolstadt and went to find him, he was gone. While I was away, he had become ill, gravely ill, and gone home to his family.'

It was at this point that Victor himself, dressed in sober black for church, came across the lawn towards us, smiling up at the terrace. I greeted him, yet, as I called down to him the sun was crossed by a cloud, the light changed, a darkness fell over the garden.

Later the party for church, Hugo's parents Mr and Mrs Feltham, his Lucy and their sons, Victor and Elizabeth Frankenstein and myself walked pleasantly through the fields to the service. Once it was over and we had knelt for a little while in private prayer, as is customary, we left with the rest of the congregation – all but Victor, who remained on his knees in the pew. I do not know how long the black-clad figure remained thus as we waited for him outside. His wife did not comment on her husband's long praying, no one else cared to refer to it, though I noted Lucy Feltham had some difficulty in preventing her sons from remarking about their delayed dinner. Eventually, Victor gravely joined us and we returned to the house, he very silent as we went. The older Mrs Feltham told us only a cold repast was provided. She was one of the school who held that the servants of a house, too, should keep the Sabbath as a day of rest. Hugo asked if she would have any objection to our spending the afternoon by the river bank and then she laughed and said she felt a day of rest need not mean a day of misery and long faces, with children trapped in the house as if in prison, doing nothing but read the Bible. What better way, she demanded, to turn a natural heathen child into a grown-up heathen in earnest?

So that afternoon the younger members of the party repaired to the river bank. It was there I heard for the first time from Victor's lips the name of Maria Clementi.

THREE

Even now, I recall vividly the ladies on the river bank in their light dresses, the sparkling of that narrow brilliant piece of water, and the fringe of mighty trees overhung by the sun on the opposite bank. I almost hear the laughter of the children, see the two bigger boys, trousers rolled up, paddling with their fishing-nets in the shallows, watch Elizabeth Frankenstein beside them, holding her skirt high with one hand and leading her own little boy to wade in the sparkling stream.

Lucy Feltham sat apart from us, surrounded by that clutter of articles ladies feel compelled to carry with them on afternoons – a hat, some salve in case of stings and bites, apples for the horses on the way home. Hugo, Victor and I sat on the grass a little further off, by request of the ladies who preferred to be at a distance from Hugo's old pipe, which he now puffed at, sending a plume of smoke up through the crystalline air, watching it waft over the water to diffuse, at last, into the trees beyond. We sat in contented silence until Victor turned to me, saying, 'Jonathan, after our conversation last night a thought came to me. I wonder if you would be interested in joining me in a scientific project I have in view?'

'I should be more than happy to consider it,' I responded warmly. Hugo, glad to have been the author of a new friendship, beamed at both of us. 'The two cleverest men of my acquaintance in alliance,' he said. 'An interesting prospect.'

'You do me too much justice,' I told him and knew I spoke the truth. I have always had a certain facility, but my own gifts, compared with Victor's detailed learning and wide-ranging, speculative ability, were as nothing. Where he roved freely, I toddled after him like a little child.

Victor told us, 'The matter concerns Miss Maria Clementi, of whom I am sure you have heard.' We had. Who, at that time, had not? One spring she had arrived in London to appear at Drury Lane and taken the town by storm as Polly Peachum in *The Beggar's Opera*. On one occasion six thousand people arrived at the theatre to purchase tickets and the manager, fearing riot, had called the militia to keep order. She was invited everywhere, mobbed everywhere she went. A man, it was rumoured, fell and fatally cracked his skull in Bond Street one day because, trying to see into Miss Clementi's carriage as it passed, he had stood on a friend's shoulders, fallen off and hit his head against the corner of a building. When she sang her voice was so pure and sweet and lifted to the high notes of the songs so effortlessly that she might have been a bird. Her charming face and figure and her elegant dancing were just as captivating – her grace, lightness and suppleness were an angel's, not a mortal woman's. I had seen her as Polly Peachum, and been enraptured, coming home in a daze with the memory of her thistledown body and her enchanting voice. I had become, as my landlady Mrs Downey frankly told me, a slave to Maria Clementi. And so, I told her, were all the men in London. To which she replied rather tartly, 'I don't wonder at it, for they all know Miss Clementi cannot speak, and perhaps that is a state all men would prefer in women.'

For Maria Clementi was dumb. She could sing most beautifully in several languages, yet she had no other power of communication at all. Report had it that she could generally understand what was said to her, though when she could not, a sweet yet uncomprehending smile would cross her face. There was apparently no organic reason for her silence. At one time some had claimed she pretended to be dumb for reasons of her own. But this ceased after a performance when she had come too close to the flaring lamps at the foot of the stage and flames had caught the gauzy dress she wore. Then, for moments, as the orchestra ceased to play and screams and cries arose in the audience, the graceful figure of Maria Clementi stood there engulfed in fire, and though her face bore an expression of the utmost terror and her two hands grasped at her throat, no sound, no scream or plea for help came from her lips. The figure was only seconds later smothered by a cloak fetched from the side of the stage. Miss Clementi was mercifully largely unhurt. But all knew then that if she had been capable of making any sound, that would have been the moment she must have done so.

Whether because of her affliction or merely as a result of her own temperament, the singer had an excellent personal reputation. Our stage was then, as *The Journal* put it, 'tinsel'. At the time we had in England no dramatists worth the name, and, while on the Continent they had their Webers, Rossinis, Bellinis, musicians of the utmost genius, we had few composers either. We had instead performances of *Macbeth* with mimes and dances between the acts, the spectacle of Master Betty 'the infant Roscius' and his tribe playing Hamlets and Ophelias at the age of nine before audiences of such unparalleled noisiness and coarseness that foreigners turned away in horror.

Oh, those Columbinas, Lucindas and Aphrodites – more prized for their bosoms and legs than their talent – Oh, those Romeos and Juliets, played as ballet-burlettas, those King Lears acted by children! We pined for the days of dramas played by men such as Garrick, for musical performances, grave – or gay – which a man could watch without the interruptions of a ballet, a clog-dance, a hornpipe, a low comedian or an exhibition of whistling, put on as if for children needing constant variety without meaning.

Plainly, in this atmosphere of folly and craving for novelty, a young, beautiful and adulated actress might lose her head. Yet Miss Clementi contrived in such a poor environment to bring some inspiration, some artistry, to the London stage.

By all accounts she lived quietly with a loyal lady companion and attended church regularly, though never going to the same church twice, since any church she might attend regularly would be mobbed by her admirers. She steered clear of society, in the main, took no lovers and stayed away from those haunts some actresses love to visit – the race courses, prize fights, gambling-houses, places no decent woman would frequent. Perhaps her affliction protected her from these follies.

Hearing Victor mention Miss Clementi's name at first surprised me. Then I thought I understood his reasons and asked, 'Do you wish to try to restore her voice?'

'Restore it or perhaps produce a voice she has never had,' he answered. 'Yes – that is my ambition. If successful the attempt would of course greatly benefit Miss Clementi, enabling her to lead a normal life among her fellows. But there is more – and this is why I would wish you to join me in my efforts, Jonathan. Imagine – just imagine – the information to be gained from studying a hitherto voiceless person (except when she sings the words of others on the stage) slowly gaining the power of speech. What might we not learn of grammar, of the meanings of words and their implications, simply by being present as the mute woman began to speak? Imagine studying an adult person who would be able to tell us all that passed in her mind as she achieved speech! Such a chance might arrive only once in a lifetime.'

'As scientific experiments go,' Hugo said robustly, 'it would be by no means unpleasant, a good deal less nasty then cutting up an eyeball or playing with noxious gases, for example. Many a man would pay guineas for the chance of sitting in a room with Miss

Clementi for any reason. You are a bachelor, Jonathan.
I advise you strongly to take up this burden.'

I assured him I knew my duty; if my studies compelled
me to enter the society of one of London's most beautiful
and admired women, I would not shirk it. I then turned
to Victor and asked him how the attempt to find Miss
Clementi's voice had come about.

He told me, 'I visited a performance by Miss Clementi
some months ago. It was a piece based on a theme from
the *Commedia dell'arte*, vulgarly done and redeemed
only by Miss Clementi's performance. I knew of course
of the dreadful incident of the fire at the theatre and of
Miss Clementi's complete inability to make any sound,
even when in extreme pain and danger. It came to
me that her being unable to speak did not merely
shut her out from communication with her fellow
creatures, but could imperil her in situations where
she could not appeal for help. I was seized with pity
for this poor young creature, who, for all her gifts and
beauty, lacks that one faculty we all possess, use daily
and take completely for granted.

'Consequently I wrote to her, saying that I understood
she had sought help from many sources and that whatever advice or treatment she had received had proved
useless, but that I thought and hoped I might be able
to help her, train her, to learn to speak.

'I said I would be more than happy to arrange some
meetings between us to make the attempt, if she would
do me the honour of agreeing. There was a silence at
first, until some ten days later when her companion,
a respectable woman of about forty, the widow of a
captain who fought against Napoleon, I heard, called at

my house. She told me that since the fire the lady, Miss Clementi, had been afflicted with melancholy. At first when asked its cause she had refused to respond in the manner she used, but the sadness persisted and in the end her companion asked her if her dumbness was the cause. Then she sighed and nodded her head, pointing sadly at her throat. The companion, Mrs Jacoby, rediscovered my letter and asked Miss Clementi if she would like help in finding a voice. Receiving her approval she came to visit me. It emerged they had both attended a lecture I had given on the structure of languages and the relationships between one tongue and another.'

'At the Royal Society in June,' I interjected. 'I read of it. It was a most excellent occasion, was it not; the room packed with the most brilliant men and women in London, both eminent scientists and the fashionable? I believe the King himself attended, Victor. Is that no so?'

'His Majesty did me that honour,' Victor agreed.

'And have you met Miss Clementi?' I asked.

Victor was rueful. 'I have, on one occasion, but we made little progress. This is my reason for asking for your help, Jonathan. I should dearly like someone with your gifts and knowledge to help me.'

'What is Miss Clementi like?' demanded Hugo.

'Very beautiful,' Victor said. 'And refined, quietly dressed and beautifully mannered. She has so far visited me only once and then, alas, in spite of all my best efforts, she only sighed, tried to speak, sighed, made another, unsuccessful attempt. In the end, she looked at me with such an air of sadness and failure it was quite heartbreaking. She gazed at me as if I held the key to some door she could not open for herself. If you could attend our meetings, Jonathan, study them, and reveal your observations to me, I would be most happy.'

Flattered and full of enthusiasm, I agreed wholeheartedly to Victor's suggestion and we settled that the next time Miss Clementi visited him in London I would be present. Two months, however, elapsed before our first encounter took place.

During August I stayed with my family in Nottingham. It was said that Miss Clementi and her companion were at a spa in Germany, where she was resting after the strains of her earlier season in London and before a Continental tour. I returned to London in late September, but by that time Miss Clementi had begun her visits to Austria, Germany and Italy, where she was rapturously received.

Back in London I continued to work quietly on my dictionary of the Aramaic tongue, that vast and demanding task I had begun with all the enthusiasm of youth some five years before and which now, many years after its inception, was nearing completion and eagerly awaited by Mr Hathaway, who would publish it.

It was during this period of quiet study that I mentioned to Mrs Downey Victor's suggestion of helping him find a cure for Maria Clementi. I must explain I had dwelt in her narrow house in Gray's Inn Road for two years, occupying a pair of rooms on the floor immediately below the servants' bedrooms. It was a modest household. I was the only lodger; Mrs Downey and her seven-year-old daughter Flora had their bedrooms on the floor below my own, and we sat and took our meals together in the rooms on the ground floor. Mrs Downey, the widow of a solicitor, was herself twenty-eight years old, only a year younger than myself, and this put us on confidential terms.

There are those who might question the propriety of a young widow, alone but for the child and the servants, taking a bachelor of her own age as a lodger. Indeed, at the time there were those who criticized our arrangement. Nevertheless, it suited us very well. Mrs Downey, though poor, was of a good family notorious since Elizabeth's time for going its own way without concern for the opinions of others. In our household there was no need to state that men and women were honourable by nature, needing no duennas, chaperones or magistrates to guide their conduct. This assertion of freedom was characteristic perhaps of the age we lived in, which still had vestiges of the old libertarian thinking of the previous century. The narrow-minded and suspicious might have said I should not have spent so many evenings alone with Mrs Downey in her comfortable parlour at the back of the house – the dining-room being the room closer to the street. But as a man with loving sisters I was accustomed to and enjoyed the company of women, for, if less weighty and informed, it is often more lively and civilised than that of men. Indeed, we often joked of being like brother and sister. To put it bluntly I believe I was lonely and so, I think, was she. Thus we drifted into the habit, when neither had other plans for the evening, into sitting together while she sewed or mended and I read.

At the time of which I speak it was late summer. We had both but recently returned to London, I having been in Nottingham and she having spent August with her sister and brother-in-law, Mr and Mrs Frazer, in Scotland. So one evening when we were together I mentioned my expectation that now I was back in London a meeting between Miss Maria Clementi and Victor Frankenstein might take place and that I might be present. I explained the reasons for this meeting but instead of expressing interest Mrs Downey raised her head from a little dress she was making for her daughter and gravely said to me, 'Perhaps I should not take the liberty of commenting, but if you will allow me, Mr Goodall, to speak to you as a sister might, I must admit this affair makes me uneasy on your behalf. I do not wish to impugn Mr Frankenstein, for I have never heard anything but good of him from your lips or those of others. Miss Clementi is also reputed to be a most excellent woman. But I am afraid this scientific attempt to restore Miss Clementi's speech alarms me, though I do not know why. Please be cautious and forgive me for producing warnings, like Cassandra, with no reasons for them.'

I answered, smiling, 'Then, addressing you as a brother might, Mrs Downey, I think you should find some.'

She sighed, let her sewing fall into her lap and gazed at me earnestly, frowning. 'Well then,' she said, 'and risking your disapproval, I will say I do not altogether trust Miss Clementi's mute tongue.'

'You heard of the occasion when her dress caught fire and she was still not able to speak or cry out,' I pointed out.

'I did,' she agreed, and here her tone took on the tone of a lawyer, perhaps that of her late husband, 'but you will not deny I'm sure that a sudden shock may strike some people dumb, just as some people instinctively shout and cry out. Nevertheless, that is not what perturbs me. I merely wonder if she is wilfully dumb; if she does not understand our language and does not wish that to be known; if indeed, she is truly mute.'

'That may be so,' I said, 'but if by chance she could speak, but will not, is that any reason for your anxiety – which I much appreciate – on my account?'

'There are no reasons I can express,' she told me. 'I feel only you may be entering deep waters.'

'Men enter deep waters in pursuit of knowledge and truth,' I replied – too lightly, too arrogantly, I now know. 'If we all stayed perpetually in the shallows, near the shore, few discoveries would be made.'

My landlady picked up her sewing again, but only looked at it with a puzzled frown. She said, to the little red dress she was making, rather than to me, 'I am a little surprised by what you told me of Mr Frankenstein spending such a long time on his knees in the church after you had all attended the service. Some twenty minutes I think you said he spent alone in the church.'

'An unusual criticism to make of a man,' I responded, 'that he spent too long praying in a church.'

'Not a criticism,' she said, 'but to me that indicates a heavy conscience.'

'Oh!' I think I exclaimed, and I believe I threw myself back in my chair impatiently, as if I were truly arguing with one of my sisters. 'How you women twist a man's behaviour – put in a bad light anything which removes itself from the narrow well-trodden track. What you do not know you fear. While we men must live to extend the boundaries, explore, discover –'

Cordelia replied, with restraint, 'Perhaps you are right, Mr Goodall. I am sorry if my comments have offended you.' And she began to sew again, diligently this time, and, noting that my further attempts at conversation were not well met, I took myself off to bed.

I own, and I am ashamed to admit it now, that I entertained the half-pleased thought that what my dear Mrs Cordelia Downey most feared about my future meeting with Miss Clementi was the effect the other lady's beauty and charm might have on me – that though, in sport, we referred to each other as brother and sister, the delightful Mrs Downey was, in fact, jealous! Fool that I was, retiring in vanity to my bed! Jealous or no, Mrs Downey's impression that involvement with Victor Frankenstein and Maria Clementi might prove dangerous to me was to prove all too true.

As I write this memoir I sometimes forget how young we all were at the time. Neither Hugo, Victor nor I had yet reached thirty; Cordelia was twenty-eight and Maria Clementi only twenty-four. Not only were we young (though old enough to know better, I admit), but we were still tainted with the spirit of the Bastille and all the new thought which had swept over Europe since. Crowns and kingdoms and all established order had toppled during the Napoleonic era. Sceptre and crown had come tumbling down so why should we not throw overboard all we did not like and make our world anew, in the light of pure reason? Why could we not discover more, understand more and change the world according to our new-found knowledge? Let us, we thought, treat our world like an old house – tear down the ancient hangings, brush away the cobwebs, fling wide the windows, allow in the pure air of truth and knowledge. That was the thinking, I believe, which led me to ignore Mrs Downey's warnings. She was no philosophical reasoner, no student of her times or any other, merely a young woman of some natural intelligence and more greatness of heart, sobered early by a marriage not altogether happy, followed by widowhood, and the care of a young daughter. I, a man with a good fortune and good health, had met little hardship in my life; she, younger than myself, had been made cautious by bereavement and rearing a young child in straitened circumstance – that was the difference between us.

FOUR

And so came the afternoon in mid-October when, following a message from Victor, I set out for Chelsea to meet Maria Clementi for the first time. (This was not the occasion I mentioned earlier, when I encountered that frightening ogreish man.)

I walked from Gray's Inn Road on a pleasant bright autumn afternoon. As I got down to Chelsea the tide was coming in, lapping at the mud, shingle and stone of the shore. Craft of every kind had come upriver with the tide – there were barges, wherries, even a great sailing ship springing and bounding upriver, wind filling its sails. In those days no walk could have been more pleasant. On one side lay the river, unbanked, with all its interest, on the other, the fields and market gardens.

I was excited at the thought of joining Victor in his attempt to solve the mystery of Miss Clementi's muteness. I rejoiced at the prospect of the wider learning which might be open to us as a result of this experience.

For a scholar there is no joy to equal that of joining his mind with that of another like mind, with the intention of widening the boundaries of knowledge. Nor, I must confess, as I mounted the steps of Victor's imposing house in Cheyne Walk, was I altogether reluctant to make the acquaintance of that ornament of the stage, Maria Clementi.

Victor himself answered my knock. He let me in, his fine eyes alive with excitement and interest. I had been punctual, Maria Clementi more than punctual. 'She's here,' Victor told me and led me with his lithe, agile step through the hall, lofty and tiled in marble, up a handsome curved staircase to a small drawing-room with tall windows looking out over the road and the river.

Maria was seated in a low brocaded chair close to where a fire burned brightly in its ornate marble fireplace. She was small and very dark with a head of black curls worn quite short, almost *à la victime* or *à la guillotine*, as the women of the French Revolution named their mannish hair arrangements, though she had a small knot of curls simply dressed with red ribbons on top of her head. The tendrils framed her face, half-covering small, pretty ears. She had very dark eyes, framed with thick, dark lashes, an oval face, small straight nose and a charming, rosy mouth, curved now in a smile. She wore a simple bonnet in pale grey and a loose woollen dress in the same colour, a lace fichu lying over her shoulders and tied in a knot over her bosom. Had it not been for a posture indicating, even in repose, the strong musculature and physical control of a dancer, one might have taken her for any charming young married woman of the middle class.

Maria's eyes were cast down as I entered but she raised them to me as we were introduced. This gaze had an effect on me very different from what I expected. The eyes of Maria, as I have said, were huge, dark and very lovely. I expected her look to seduce me, win me. I had looked forward, with some enjoyment, to the effect of first meeting the eyes of Maria Clementi. Yet, as our glances met, I felt first – awe. There is what we call a 'speaking look' where the eyes alone convey their possessor's meaning and mood. This 'speaking look' is more common in women, creatures of sentiment, than in men, whose gaze is more direct and thoughtful. Maria's eyes were the opposite of 'speaking'. They were silent, as her own tongue. To look into them was to gaze into the black waters of one of those bottomless tarns of the North. One fears; one half wishes to throw oneself into those still expressionless depths; one attempts to see through the dark waters – and sees nothing. As I made greetings I wondered if the silence imposed on Maria by her dumbness had created this great, fathomless calm in her slate-coloured eyes.

As I gazed, half-mesmerised, into Maria Clementi's eyes the awe I had felt at once began to verge on fear. I knew I wished to look forever, to come closer, look again, and never cease to look.

Victor interrupted, mercifully, by proposing to introduce me to Maria's companion, Mrs Jacoby. On hearing her name, this lady stood up from the window seat and came across the room to greet me. She was a woman of about forty years old, of medium height, erect in her bearing, with a direct look and what I believe ladies call a practical bonnet. She bore the stamp of a soldier's wife who has followed her husband on many a campaign, set up house in many a place, made do in all manner of hardships and difficulties. Her forthright blue eyes met mine, perfectly civilly but saying to me, as to all the world, I believe. 'No nonsense from you, if you please.' As soon as I had bowed to her and murmured I was happy to meet her, she went back to her seat, leaving the three of us, Victor, Maria and myself, by the fire.

We all sat down, Maria in her former chair, Victor opposite her on the other side of the fireplace; I took a third chair between them. I had no idea how Victor had conducted his previous interview or how he meant to proceed, so I broke the silence, rather awkwardly, by commenting on the pleasant afternoon and saying I had walked to Chelsea from my lodgings. I spoke slowly, as if addressing a foreigner, and felt a little foolish for doing so. Maria bent her head to me, heeded me as if she understood, and when I had finished gave me a small, charming smile.

Victor, rather to my astonishment, then asked her in German if she would care to stand up and walk to the door. Maria merely gazed at him, biting her lip, seeming to be trying to understand him. Whereupon Victor addressed her in French, again asking her if she would go to the door. And Maria, smiling, stood up – and went to the door. She turned there, still smiling, asking, it would seem, for Victor's approval, which he, with a smile of great satisfaction, gave. And then he spoke to her in other languages, many of which I did not know myself, plainly asking her to do various things. In no case, except when he asked her in Italian to go to the window (which instruction he had to repeat various times before she could understand him), did she stir from her chair and do so. As this went on she gazed at him, I thought, with increasing weariness.

After this, Victor turned to me and asked, 'Curious, is it not, that Miss Clementi knows French, evidently, and some Italian and English, but no other languages?'

I nodded, a little embarrassed. Maria was with us and could understand us, yet we discussed her as if she were not present, as often happens with children or the very old or ill. This seemed stranger still when the subject was a young woman in her right mind, merely dumb. I asked, 'Have you spoken in various languages to Miss Clementi before?' And he said that he had not. I then spoke to Miss Clementi, asking her if she had known French since childhood or had learned it later in her life. She shrugged prettily, indicating she did not know – or perhaps could not understand what I was asking. Mrs Jacoby then spoke up from her window seat. 'Miss Clementi sings in all languages,' she said.

'But parrot-fashion,' Victor said. 'For apparently she understands only French and English.' Then to Maria he proposed, 'Well then, Miss Clementi, shall we try our exercises?'

He then launched into a series of consonants, as if encouraging a child to speak, 'B-b-b-b, D-d-d-d, M-m-m-m.' He urged Maria, as one would a child, to copy him. But, lips parted and showing every sign of effort in trying to do as he asked, she had no success. She made no sound at all. All I heard were pitiful exhalations of breath – and sometimes a sigh – a sad contrast to that voice I had heard at the theatre, soaring high, in the duet of Polly Peachum and Captain Macheath:

I would love you all the day
All day long we'd kiss and play.
If with me you'd fondly stray,
Over the hills and far away . . .

There was nothing of that carefree spirit now. Maria was distressed. Victor then broke off, saying nothing but looking at her reprovingly; while she became confused and a little ashamed.

Then, 'Again,' he urged. 'Let us try again.' They began again, the demonstration becoming more painful but just as futile. I knew some method would have to be developed if Maria were to find her speaking voice, and that some toil, even agony might be involved if the method were to succeed. Nevertheless Maria's increasing distress was not pleasant to see. I abandoned the painful scene by the fire and crossed to the window to speak to Mrs Jacoby, reasoning that she might, even without knowing it herself, possess some clue to the secret of Maria's locked tongue. Victor had embarked on vowels, 'A-e-i-o-u,' he pronounced. 'Come, Maria – try – try.' But she made no sound.

'So far there's been no success at all that you can see, Mrs Jacoby?' I asked.

She shook her head and replied steadily. 'We had much hoped – after Maria's time away, resting and working on the exercises – ' Her voice trailed away.

'The exercises being what is happening now?'

'And some others connected with breathing,' she told me.

'It's very mysterious,' I said. 'There is nothing organically wrong with Miss Clementi and she sings so beautifully – yet cannot speak. Tell me, Mrs Jacoby, does she never, never make any sound – cry out, sob aloud, groan, laugh? Perhaps she talks in her sleep, or makes some sound – ' And I noted as I spoke the last words that Mrs Jacoby looked at me more attentively. There was a long silence between us. She was summing me up, as she might have summed up a subaltern newly arrived in her husband's regiment. Then she said, 'Can you swear to keep a secret?' I responded that I was unwilling to swear to keep any secret when I did not know what it was.

'Well, then,' she said wryly, 'you will never know, will you?' And at this point my curiosity so much got the better of me that I said, 'If what you tell me is not a guilty secret, and will harm no one, then – I swear not to tell it.'

'Fair enough,' she said, with something of the decisiveness of the battlefield in her tone, 'then I'll tell you. I have never heard Maria Clementi speak one word or make a sound – except at night. Then I have heard her, in nightmare, calling out, crying out in fear.'

'Have you told anyone of this?' I asked her.

'Never,' she replied. 'Earlier she seemed content enough to be dumb – but lately she appears increasingly distressed by her position.'

I asked her, 'You have not told Mr Frankenstein of these cryings out, in nightmare?'

She shook her head. By now I was puzzled.

'Remember – you have promised,' she warned me.

'But Mr Frankenstein should know this.' I reproached her. 'Why do you not tell him?'

She did not reply because at that moment Victor stood and said, amiably enough, in our direction, 'I think we have had enough for today. Miss Clementi must not get too tired. I know she is to perform tonight in *Acis and Galatea*. Mrs Jacoby, if you return next week Mr Goodall and I will have had the opportunity to discuss the matter and devise some new plans.'

And thus the first consultation, if that is what I should call it, ended. Maria, I thought, looked pale. In parting, she pressed my hand gently, while Mrs Jacoby expressed goodwill and hoped she would see me at Cheyne Walk the following week.

After they left Victor bit his lip, looking anxious and thoughtful. 'Let us sit down,' he said. 'Some wine?'

I refused this and we sat down to talk. Frowning he said, 'All this is most baffling. I know she can speak. I am certain of it, I know. Sometimes I feel Miss Clementi is defying me to help her. Her efforts to produce a voice appear great, but I do not think they are great enough. I fear she may be deceiving me. As an actress, she is fully capable of miming a struggle to speak. I must – must – discover the key to open that door – or break it down.' He sighed vigorously, then said impatiently, 'I really do not understand. In all the literature there is no comparable case. And, my dear Jonathan, if only we could succeed, what might we not find out about the structure of our language and its connection with the workings of the mind?' He smacked his fist into his palm and I think if he had been another man he would have started swearing and cursing.

I felt some guilt at suppressing the information Mrs Jacoby had given me, that Maria cried out in her sleep, but I had given my word, and could see no way of breaking it. Worse, it was my impression that Mrs Jacoby had not only made me swear to keep the secret in general but specifically to keep it from Victor. This seemed absurd – why should not the whole world know Maria Clementi had some voice and particularly why should not Victor, who was dedicated to helping her? However, there was nothing I could do.

'You have established that Miss Clementi has knowledge of two languages but no others,' I said. 'That is interesting. We may assume her understanding of speech is like that of any other person. She knows these tongues she has encountered, or learned. But tell me, what is her past? Where does she come from? Who are her parents?'

'Very little is known of her,' Victor said. 'She, of course, can tell people nothing of herself. But it would seem she was found by the man who is still her impresario – whatever that may mean – in Ireland some four years ago and was taken by him to the manager of Drury Lane, the famous Mr Robert Elliston. He took her up with enthusiasm and began her career.'

'And is Maria Clementi truly her name?'

'I believe it was invented by her manager, the impresario Mr Gabriel Mortimer, in discussion with Mr Elliston,' Victor told me. 'I suppose no one knows her real name.'

'Except herself, and she cannot tell us,' I responded.

'What a strange, sad time she must have had of it, poor Miss Clementi.'

'She is a most beautiful and gifted creature,' Victor said. 'Unique. Extraordinary. Compensation enough.'

I could not answer him.

Naturally I asked Victor if Maria was able to communicate her thoughts in writing but in those days fewer could read and write than in these more enlightened times, so it was no surprise when Victor informed me that Maria was scarcely literate. I suggested to Victor, therefore, that the restoration of Miss Clementi's voice would not be harmed by learning to read and write. The study of words in their written form might help to concentrate her mind and will on speaking them out loud. And even if this was not the effect, then at least she would have the benefit of expressing herself more freely in writing. Victor showed little enthusiasm for this scheme.

Mrs Jacoby had said nothing would persuade Maria to write more than the odd scribbled word – and that she could do. He added, 'Cannot – will not – I do not know. Sweet-natured and good as she appears, I wonder if there is not something hard, uncooperative, obstinate about the girl.'

For my part, I wondered if, like many a teacher, in the momentary frustration of making no progress with a pupil, Victor was not resorting to blaming his student, instead of devising a method to encourage her.

'You cannot mean that she is a fraud – could write but will not and therefore – could speak but will not?' I asked wonderingly.

'No,' he said. 'But there must be something – some machinery – which would make her speak.'

I saw in him the ever-enthusiastic, ever-able student unable to believe there are those in the world who cannot learn. This was to him a battle which he must win. Mercifully at that moment in came his charming wife and offered us tea; Victor became more easy and the atmosphere more cordial. We began to talk rationally about finding some method to make Maria talk, deciding that one course would be to ask Maria to start by singing, then induce her to say the words of the song instead of singing them. It was a simple plan, but simplicity is sometimes effective.

We did not begin that week, or the week after, for Maria was studying a new operetta, *Hera's Revenge* by Maestro Valli and encountering difficulties with the work. Rehearsals were prolonged and, as she was also performing daily at the playhouse in another piece it was not until that gloomy afternoon in November, which I have previously described, that we met again at Cheyne Walk in the same small parlour as before.

Though the fire burned, fog from the river crept through the drawn curtains making the atmosphere in the room obscure. Once again, Mrs Jacoby, now in a thick Paisley shawl, sat by the window. Maria was in her old position by the fire, with Victor again opposite her and I between them.

Victor explained to Maria the plan that she should begin with song then modify the song into speech. She appeared to understand what was said, though she frowned a little, whether because she disliked the idea or because she secretly believed it would not work

I do not know. I said, recalling the happy evening at Old Hall in Kent when we had all so merrily sung 'Youth's the season made for joys' from Mr Gay's *The Beggar's Opera*, that I would dearly love to hear Maria sing some of the work and she cheerfully agreed.

I shall never forget, even after all that occurred later, the spectacle of that small, slender figure, standing at the fireplace as, in that thrilling voice, she began to sing the simple air, forget her beautifully shaped face and great, sad eyes turned slightly upwards, the fall of her black curls, the perfect oval of her opened mouth giving out such a glorious, effortless sound in the dull, foggy room.

Dance and sing, Time's on the wing,
Life never knows the return of spring
Let us drink and sport today,
Love with youth flies swift away.

Perhaps it was then I became fascinated by her, doomed to fulfil the dark suspicions I thought Cordelia Downey harboured concerning my motives in wishing to assist Victor in his work with Maria Clementi. I sat entranced, wishing that this perfect, untouched creature – for so she seemed to me at that time – could be mine.

A part of me, recognising danger, tried to insist it was the artist, not the woman I admired. But this was not true. I felt hopeless longing. When she finished her song I sat in awe, knowing how few men can have been so privileged as to have sat on a drab afternoon, in an ordinary room, hearing Maria sing. But I yearned for her at that moment and whatever occurred later

I cannot swear I ever lost that longing. Bluntly, she was an actress; she was mute. Both in terms of society and because of her disablement I knew she could have become unconditionally mine. I am a man. I think as men do and I am no better than the others.

Then, our efforts had to begin. The song had been well chosen for our purposes, and it ought to have been easy enough to eliminate the music from it, gradually turning the song into speech, rather like operatic recitative. Or like a chanted psalm, half-speech, half-song. This exercise, as I say, should have been easy – but was not. Maria would sing a line with perfect purity, would sing it in a minor key if required to do so, but what it seemed she could not do was take the song word by word, or make the words sound like ordinary speech. It was as though she saw words and music as one single entity and could not separate the two. Asking her to break up a phrase into its component parts was as if one required a bird to stop its song at a certain point or slow it, or repeat a phrase of its cadence. A bird could not do this; nor, apparently, could Maria.

All afternoon we laboured, altering from song to song, then attempting some psalms. But Maria could not 'drone' psalms any more than she could 'speak' songs, though her voice rose and fell like an angel's. An hour passed, then another. Victor's demands grew sharper and Maria, I thought, began to tire. At one point I glanced at Mrs Jacoby and her face told me she was regretting the exercise. As Victor felt doubt and fatigue overwhelming hope he grew ever more determined, while my role became less that of the helper and witness of the attempt, more that of one trying to contain the worst elements of the struggle. It was then that Maria, unprompted, embarked on the lament addressed to Aeneas by the deserted Queen Dido in Purcell's opera, *Dido and Aeneas*, wherein she sadly sings: 'When I am laid in earth, may my wrongs create no trouble in thy breast. Remember me – but forget my fate.'

I was entranced. I glanced at Victor who was strained and pale. He looked like a man who had been struck. Then he rallied and broke into the song, chanting unmelodically the words for her to imitate, 'My wrongs create no trouble – Remember me . . .' And Maria tried to copy him – and sang, her voice soaring to the ceiling. And 'Remember me,' said Victor in a speaking voice, and 'Remember me' sang Maria. They went over and over it until Maria followed Victor, who had once more said-sung 'Remember me', by bursting triumphantly out with the rest of the song – and concluding it. Victor sprang from his chair with an exclamation of impatience he could not control – at which poor Maria sat down abruptly, put her hands to her face and broke into dreadful, soundless sobs. Victor was at her side in an instant, kneeling at her side with his arms around her, soothing her, apologising for his behaviour: 'I have pressed you too hard. I am a villain. Forgive me – I have asked too much of you.' These were the muttered words I heard.

This scene, I must admit in my brutal Saxon way, struck me at the time as 'foreign', over-emotional, lacking in restraint. This, at any rate, was how I explained these outpourings of emotion on Victor's part, and the fact that Maria, whose tears had ceased, continued to sit bent in her chair, apparently listening to his explanations and apologies. But his words were extreme and the situation hardly suitable between a man and a woman, the man married. This was quickly perceived by the already uneasy Mrs Jacoby, who was soon close to the pair, urging Victor to his feet. She then confronted him, saying stiffly, 'I am sure Maria knows you are doing all you can to help her, but she is tired and has a performance tonight. I must take her away to rest.'

Which she did. Farewells were made and, as they left, I saw Maria turn back in the doorway fixing those great luminous eyes on Victor's with the expression, I thought, of a loved, and loving dog – then she was gone.

That look of hers alarmed me. I then told Victor I must leave myself, but he scarcely heard, I think, for he was standing by the window looking out, not down to the road, where Maria and Mrs Jacoby were departing in their carriage, but through the darkening air, across the river.

Elizabeth Frankenstein was in the hall as I left. I raised my hand to her in farewell as I walked off, but in that light, with snow falling, I saw her only as an obscure, monochromatic figure standing in her own doorway, like a ghost.

Not three minutes later came the moment when I observed that monstrous figure on the wharf, who, later, raised his accusatory arm towards the house in Cheyne Walk, howling out his grief. You may well imagine how disturbed I was at this scene, following so hard on the earlier events at Cheyne Walk.

So shaken was I by my afternoon – for, though

there was superficially nothing in it truly to disturb a young healthy man with strong nerves, I *was* disturbed – that after my diversion at the Voyagers' Club on my return home, I quietly took my place by Cordelia Downey's parlour fire, saying nothing about the events of the afternoon. What I might have told her was too nebulous and too disturbing. And she herself was tired after a trying domestic day and her daughter's invalid demands, for little Flora, was in bed with a cold.

So we chatted for a little time and then I took my candle up to my room. There the idea came to me that if we, Victor and I, were really to assist Maria to speak, then I would do well to keep a record of our procedures. Whether Victor himself were doing this or not, I reasoned, in such a cases, two accounts can be more useful than one. So, taking a pile of paper and a pen I sat shivering (for my fire had not been lit) and, heading the first page of my account with the date, November the 11th, I then solidly set down, in every detail, what had occurred that day. And throughout the horrible events I shall go on to describe I continued to make this daily record; which is why I am now able to give a complete account, from my point of view, of what passed. You may picture me, during that winter of 1825 in my small sitting-room on the second floor, furnished barely, with table, chair, chest, and sometimes without a fire, often chilled cold, sometimes shivering with horror and incredulity, as I made my recording. Many times as I wrote, I thought I was mad.

FIVE

I woke unrefreshed after a troubled night, my sleep penetrated by repeated strains of music, by the anguished face of Maria, by the howls of that great creature on the quay. Just before I woke, I dreamed that the sad expression of Maria as she tried, hopelessly, to speak, and the twisted, beetle-browed face of the creature on the quay changed places. On Maria's face I saw ferocity and torment, while the great savage man's expression as he pointed North and howled was replaced by the pleading countenance of Maria. Unable to sleep longer, I rose, dressed and was downstairs before the sun was fully up.

Yet evidently I had not risen before Victor, for not long after, I was handed a note which had been delivered earlier by one of his servants. It said only, 'Come to me early, I beg you. I must speak to you.'

'I must go early to Mr Frankenstein's,' I told Cordelia, who was pouring tea.

She mused, 'Mr Hathaway is waiting for your dictionary.'

True enough, for, as I have remarked, my friend David Hathaway, respected bookseller and printer, was very desirous of having my dictionary of Aramaic to print and publish and I had all too often put forward the date on which I was to deliver it to him. Perhaps I ought to have seen Mrs Downey's criticism as a warning rather than a reproach. In general I lack the usual masculine ability to ignore the voices of women. Men ask, why listen to the voices of those ill-educated creatures, whose limited intellectual capacity leads them to concern themselves only with bonnets and the dishonesty of laundrywomen? True enough – yet in practice I cannot always ignore the comments of women for they can often come to wise conclusions based on no experience or information whatsoever. I have often wondered how this can be. However, this time I accepted neither reproach nor warning.

'So, Mrs Downey, you disapprove still of the attempt to help Maria Clementi?' I enquired.

What woman asked for a comment will deny you one? She instantly responded with a question, 'Would you be so concerned for her if she were a nasty old man with a beard?'

At this I laughed and she crossly added, 'You know nothing of the past.'

'Miss Clementi, being mute, is hardly in a position to account for her past life,' said I.

'I did not make myself clear. I spoke of the past life of Mr Frankenstein,' said she.

'Mrs Downey,' I answered her, 'I do not think, with

all respect, that you know at all what you are talking about.'

Happily this exchange ended when a maid came in to announce the coalman had arrived bringing the wrong supplies.

As Victor's note was urgent, I went straight to Cheyne Walk in a hired carriage. There the butler, a reliable-looking middle-aged man, led me straight to Victor's study. He turned from the window where he had been standing with a paper in his hand and declared, in great agitation, 'See this! It is a letter from Mrs Jacoby saying Miss Clementi will come here no more! The visits are tiring, says the woman, and each defeat plunges Maria deeper into despondency. Maria cannot mean it! She is under the influence of her foul companion. It may be she does not even know what that woman is doing in her name. We must go to her, Jonathan.'

This vehemence bewildered me. I did not find it so strange that Maria had become discouraged by our lack of progress. And Victor's impatience at the end of the last meeting had caused her distress. It seemed all too probable she had decided to discontinue the efforts to help her regain or discover her powers of speech. I attempted to reason with Victor, saying, 'Victor – Victor – my dear fellow – let us think calmly what to do.'

'We must go to her immediately,' was all he said.

'Victor,' I said, 'we cannot assume that this letter does not convey Miss Clementi's own decision.'

'That is nonsense – nonsense,' he said passionately. 'She has been influenced. We must go to her.'

As I have said, I saw ample reason why Miss Clementi might herself want to end her lessons, not least of which was the very ferocity of passion about them that Victor now demonstrated. Nor was she a lady of leisure who might spend the afternoon with Victor and consider herself as well entertained as if she had spent the time visiting on other ladies for tea and conversation. Each night Maria Clementi faced an audience to whom she was a goddess – and knew no doubt that if she began to disappoint her worshippers they would soon enough become her revilers. Such is the nature of fame. But Victor's agitation was so dreadful that, to calm him, I unwisely agreed to go with him to call at Maria's house.

To my alarm he proposed to start immediately. It was barely nine o'clock. I pointed out that it was too early to call, and that a stage performer may sleep later into the morning than other folk, but he would have none of this. He ordered his carriage to be brought to the door and only half an hour later we were at the tall house in Russell Square that Maria had taken, I assume, because of its proximity to the theatre. This was an imposing dwelling, and very well furnished. As I had anticipated Maria had not yet risen and we were shown into a handsome dining-room decorated in the Chinese style, with an oriental carpet on the floor and many charming vases in niches round the room.

Mrs Jacoby, who was arranging a handsome lacquer table for breakfast, greeted us with some surprise. She was beginning, politely, to offer us some hospitality when Victor, still standing in the doorway, (the man-servant behind him vainly asking if he might take his coat,) immediately burst out, 'Mrs Jacoby – what is the meaning of this letter? Do you know what you are doing? I will not accept the termination of my efforts to help Miss Clementi!'

Mrs Jacoby, plainly trying to contain anger at his tone, replied coolly, 'Mr Frankenstein. I wrote to you because Miss Clementi indicated to me that she no longer wishes to continue to visit you. She does not feel your efforts are helping her and she finds your manner unsympathetic.'

'How can you tell?' he demanded. 'You put words into her mouth because she cannot speak. Let me see her.'

'She is in her room,' Mrs Jacoby told him.

'Then I shall wait until she descends,' he said and sat down at the table. I began to regret very much I had not prevented Victor from making this assault on the house in Russell Square. I had believed that once we had arrived he would moderate his behaviour, but this was certainly not the case. I could not comprehend this rude and bullying behaviour; he seemed a different man. I suggested we might leave and find a better time to talk to Maria.

Mrs Jacoby regarded me with some scorn, as Victor responded instantly, 'No. This matter must be settled now.'

Then she allowed her anger to show. 'There is no "must" about it, Mr Frankenstein. Miss Clementi does not wish to continue her meetings with you. I wrote on her behalf to inform you of that fact. You have come here, uninvited, at an early hour and settled down to wait for her without invitation, and I must confess I find your behaviour unseemly. Mr Frankenstein – Miss Clementi is a young woman without family, unprotected in the world, whose only resources come from what she earns, by her own talents, which she must preserve. Her mental equilibrium is therefore essential to her. She has told you her wishes. Please respect them.'

'You wish to keep her away from the world, no doubt,' Victor said. 'Her talents are your fortune, and I suppose you want to keep them to yourself. Perhaps it would be unfortunate for you if Miss Clementi recovered her voice and were able to meet the world on equal terms. I must see her, to learn from her what she truly wants.'

Victor's language was shocking and I opened my mouth to restore him to order, only to find Mrs Jacoby before me, and perfectly equal to the task.

'It appears you have parted from your reason, Mr Frankenstein, and I hope for your sake the condition is temporary. But while you are in this state I do not want you in this house. You will kindly leave.'

And at that point Maria, fresh in a simple morning gown of pale yellow, her short curls piled on her head, entered with a charming smile, apparently unaware of any troubling situation. She went to kiss Mrs Jacoby, then offered her hand to Victor and myself.

As she did this, and before Victor could speak, as he evidently wished to, Mrs Jacoby said to Maria in a gentle voice, 'Maria, my dear. Mr Frankenstein has come to ask you to reconsider your intention to break off your lessons with him. Will you let him know in some manner that your decision not to continue is firm, and your own?'

But Maria did nothing, only gazing at Victor, gently smiling while he stood still, his eyes fixed on hers, his face very pale.

'Maria,' said Mrs Jacoby, 'please indicate your wishes to Mr Frankenstein.'

As this went on I heard the front door bang and then some steps in the hall. The dining-room door then opened and in stepped as obnoxious a fellow as I have seen for many a long day. They say you should not judge a man by his appearance, but one glance at this person said all there was to say about him. He was clad from top to toe in a dreadful shade of burgundy. His trousers were too tight, his boots too glossy, the black hat under his arm too high. His face was long and sallow, his head covered with oiled black curls. He had weary dark eyes, of the kind which have looked on too many dawns without benefit of sleep. He showed very white teeth as he stood, smiling, or rather, posing in the doorway, as if for his portrait. This was Gabriel Mortimer, Maria's impresario, fop, dandy – and villain.

He looked very coolly at Victor and myself as Mrs Jacoby introduced us. She did not mention the reason for our presence. Mortimer nodded to each of us and told Mrs Jacoby, 'I have come with information about Maestro Valli's *Hera's Revenge*. The composer wants the order of three scenes changed and nothing will persuade him to leave matters as they are.'

Victor, ignoring Mortimer completely, urged Maria, 'Please, Maria. Come to me again next week. I implore you – for your own sake, do as I say.'

And Maria – nodded!

'Maria!' cried Mrs Jacoby in reproachful tones. Could it be true, as Victor believed, that she had indeed attempted to force a separation between the poor mute woman and the man who might save her from perpetual silence?

'Thank God,' cried Victor. 'Oh – thank God!' – and Maria smiled.

Some chilly adieux followed and Victor, nodding briefly at Mortimer, left the room. Having said goodbye to Mortimer myself, I was bidding Mrs Jacoby farewell when she went with me to the door, saying in a low voice, 'Will you be at Frankenstein's when Maria next goes there?' and I replied that I hoped I would.

'Try,' she said then. 'I would be most grateful if you would attend.'

Uncertain within myself, I agreed I would do my best to do what she asked. But as I joined Victor in the street I wondered what role Captain Jacoby's widow was playing in this strange affair. Victor, as we parted outside the house, questioned nothing; he was all happiness, overjoyed that Maria had come back to him.

Nevertheless, I was puzzled. Was Mrs Jacoby a female villain, controlling the life of Maria for her own reasons? Or had Maria told her at some point that she did want to cease her lessons with Victor and then simply changed her mind? Where did the unsavoury Gabriel Mortimer figure in the affair? If Mrs Jacoby were indeed a villain, and Mortimer pretty certainly another, in what dreadful situation was Maria placed, helplessly, between that pair? I thought Maria's innocence must have been preserved, despite daily contact with this dreadful fellow, only because she could not converse with him.

As I walked back to my lodgings, another thought occured to me. I am a virtuous man now, to the extent of my poor powers and even at the time of which we speak I was not indulging myself in dalliance with women. In fact I had made a resolution that before the hot blood of youth turned to the thin blood of debauchery I would make what efforts I could to mend my ways, for no sight is more repellent than an aging man creeping about after women when he should be at his work or his own fireside. Yet I recalled how often in the past I had played the old game of creeping downstairs from a bedroom, shoes in my hand, then opening the front door from the inside, slamming it as if I had just come in, and then – on with the shoes and – lo – entering the parlour comes honest young Jack Trueblood, calling with an open smile just as if he had not spent all night in that very house, upstairs in bed with Polly Perkins.

I could not be sure Gabriel Mortimer's entry that morning had not been an appearance of the kind I have described. I had not heard the bell ring or the knocker knock. I had not heard a servant go to the door. Perhaps, then, he had a key to the house but that would hardly be suitable – a man with the key to a house inhabited by two ladies? But if he had been in the house all along and only crept down from upstairs? What a picture that raised in the mind! My chivalrous soul – or, rather, my jealous soul – roused up on Maria's behalf. Was Mortimer Mrs Jacoby's lover? That would make her predicament, mute and unbefriended, except by that pair, even more frightful, her position as pawn in their game more frightful still.

SIX

I was not at the next meeting between Victor and Maria, for the very next day came a message from my sister Arabella, desiring me to return home immediately, for my father was very ill. And so I galloped back to Nottingham at all speed, through mud and ice, to find my father gravely affected by a congestion of the lungs. Mercifully this abated and he turned the corner, though his recovery was slow. He was better, though still weak, six weeks later when the Christmas festivities began.

There was much visiting to and fro between neighbours, and some twenty at our table for the Christmas feast. During this time, as my father recovered his health, it was incumbent on me to play the head of the family and keeper of the estate. Thus I was fully occupied with many things, from the tenants' quarter-day payments to escorting my sisters hither and yon.

It was at a ball ten miles off, whence I had gone wearily in a carriage, that my sister Arabella consented to be the wife of our neighbour's son, Dudley Hight, a good fellow (though I thought him dull) trained for the law. And just after the New Year my younger sister Anna threatened to marry the curate of our parish church and was dispatched hastily to Northumberland with my father's sister, who had joined us for the festivities and was returning there.

Between suitors, desirable and undesirable, broken hedges, rents, leases, parties, hunting and the entertainment of friends and kin I was held, pleasantly, in Nottingham until the middle of January, though London, my studies – and David Hathaway – called. Truth to tell, I discovered my only real desire to return to London was to rejoin Mrs Downey for I found I missed her presence, her nice looks and charming companionship, and began to wonder if Nottingham might not have been even more enjoyable had she been there. I could open my heart and mind to her even more freely than I could to my family and I imagined her daughter, little Flora, child of the bad air and adulterated foodstuffs of the city, benefiting from all we had in Nottingham. These thoughts even interrupted my sleep as I imagined my charming landlady in the place I loved most in all the world.

Meanwhile my comfortable country life went on – had to go on, for tomorrow I must see Mr Such-and-Such about the wood, next day we would hunt, the day after that there was a visit, the day after the bailiff would come about planting, and so it went on.

It was a letter from my friend Hugo Feltham which dug me from my rut and brought me speedily back to London. This letter, delivered by a muddy cart from the village, arrived one day just as I had come in from the fields for my breakfast. I read it standing before the fire, warming my bones, while Arabella cut slices of beef for my father. We had gone up in the world but still kept to the old country habit of good beer, good meat and good bread for breakfast, taken after the house had been up and doing for many hours: even a lady who did not come down for breakfast was held to be sick, a man who failed to arrive was taken to be on his deathbed and past praying for.

I was surprised to receive a letter from Hugo, no lover of pen and paper. I have known him ride ten miles to communicate a message in person rather than send a letter or note. Consequently, when I opened the letter I knew some serious matter was afoot.

'My dearest Jonathan,' the letter read, 'I have been hesitating for some time whether to write to you. But Lucy urges me to do so and we both agree you must be told what is happening as regards our valued friend Victor, whom I know we both love. Alas, all is not well with him. I am no penman, as you know, Jonathan, so I must put the matter bluntly – Victor is in love with Miss Maria Clementi. He haunts the theatre after her performances; he buys her gifts which, apparently, she receives; he visits her frequently at Russell Square. Poor Elizabeth has twice been dispatched to us by Victor, who tries to conceal what he is doing, but Elizabeth is undeceived and just now she has been here, with us at Old Hall, for a week. She has now resolved to return to London to be with her husband, however distressing his behaviour. Lucy and I have offered what help we can and have said that if she finds her situation intolerable

she must come again to us. I am detained here for the
present and think you could be useful in this matter.
In short, I ask you to go to Victor and attempt to find
out the nature of his relations with Miss Clementi and
tell him of the distress he is causing his wife. My dear
old Jonathan, you know this is not the kind of task one
man lightly hands to another, but for the sake of poor
Elizabeth Frankenstein, and Victor himself also – will
you assist?'

I was shocked by this message, after a moment I was
still more shocked by my own stupidity. It should
have been plain to me, witnessing Victor's agitation
when Maria threatened to give up her lessons with
him and his violent behaviour at Russell Square later,
that I was not observing a scientist but a man in the
throes of passion for a woman. Such was my respect
for Victor's intellectual gifts I had been blind to conduct
which, in anyone else, I would have seen plainly as
amorous folly.

Then, I reflected what a dreadful task lay ahead of me.
I should have to appeal to Victor to give up Maria for the
sake of his wife and child, not to mention for the sake of
his own reputation. Then most probably there would be
an interview with Mrs Jacoby, and Heaven only knew
how that little causerie would turn out. The vision was
so afflicting, I believe, standing by the fireplace, I may
have sworn aloud. At any rate Arabella uttered a startled
sound and my father uttered a warning 'Hmph!'

But Hugo had appealed to me, doubt at Lucy's
instigation, and I had no choice but to tackle this
unpleasant duty. No point in delaying – I packed rapidly,
said my farewells and took the London Road, which

was mercifully dry for the time of year. I thus reached London by nightfall of the same day and, having made arrangements for the return of my horse to Nottingham, set off straight away for the theatre where Maria was appearing. I thought that if matters were as described in Hugo's letter, I might well find Victor there.

The house was packed. By bullying and bribing I managed to find a place standing at the back of the theatre and so saw, through a crowd of heads, the last act of *Hera's Revenge*. It did not fall short of the traditions of the London stage at the time, which is to say it was trumpery and trivial as a prize at a fair. Nevertheless, as the curtain went up on the slender, lonely figure of Maria Clementi, hands clasped in front of her, playing Jove's young lover Constantia and singing a pretty song expressing her love for the god, the audience, unable to contain itself (and lacking that restraint which these days we prefer to observe), stood, shouted, and cried out in delight. There were calls of 'Brava, brava.' Having completed her song, Maria began to dance. That vision will never leave me – a gold-clad form, gossamer-light yet strong as a young aspen – white arms raised above a beautifully poised head, garlanded with flowers – her grace, her purity, her loveliness. How the men standing about me at the back of the theatre cheered and groaned. It was easy to see how Victor Frankenstein, like so many others, could feel passion for Maria. Who would not?

The dance ended and some black-faced dancers came on, for little dramatic reason, naming themselves African Sal and Dusty Bob and began some silly dance from the plantations, he in ragged trousers, she in a print dress with a rag tied round her head. Then came the implausible arrival of Jove, who appeared on the scene to court Constantia dressed as a golden ram (if sense were lacking in the piece the costumes and scenery were outstanding). With the entrance of his jealous wife Hera, rightly suspecting his plan to seduce Constantia, a duet began between the pair.

At this point I realised that, Victor, who was not in the theatre as far as I could see, might have elected to arrive before the end of the performance and gone directly to join what I was sure would be a mighty crowd behind the scenes. So I began pushing my way from the theatre, causing more protest, even, than when I had pushed my way in. Just before I left I turned to see a new backdrop, an English landscape with meadows and sheep. Against it stood Jove, Hera and a full chorus, all singing. In front of them was Maria, in her golden shift, a coronet of flowers in her hair, singing like a bird, with no harshness, yet clearly audible against the chorus of other singers. It was a pretty spectable.

I went into the alley beside the theatre and found the stage door. As the result of a bribe and a claim of aquaintanceship with Miss Maria Clementi, I was ushered behind the scenes and in to a crowded greenroom. I spotted a marquis, an ambassador and many other dignitaries. There were ladies of fashion with plumes in their hair and officers in uniform just come from their duties. In one corner a parrot screamed in a golden cage and in another two large hounds sat perfectly still, looking a great deal more dignified than the people around them. But there was no sign of Victor. My eyes sought, and found, Mrs Jacoby. She wore a black silk dress. Then Maria entered with other members of the cast – the crowd opened to receive her, then closed again. I thought, wrongly, as it turned out, that if I could get to Mrs Jacoby I might have a private word with her about whatever state of affairs existed between Frankenstein and Maria. But, push as I might against shoulders clad in silk, red tunics or black wool, I could get no closer than the second rank of worshippers.

Whatever my suspicions of Mrs Jacoby I was forced to admire her composure and competence. She was, after all, Maria's voice. For many years now she had had to judge what Maria wanted to say, and should or should not say. In that sense she had been a true support to the young woman. She now stood beside her, dealing with myriad comments and enquiries. I heard her say, 'Miss Clementi finds this role taxing, but less so than the more sombre role of Dido in Purcell's *Dido and Aeneas*, in which part you have no doubt seen her. Miss Clementi thanks your lordship for his most kind comments. Miss Clementi exercises at a barre, as dancers do in Russia, for one hour each day.'

At one point she caught my eye, and, I think, controlled a startled expression at seeing me. I inclined my head but saw no purpose in staying longer; it would have been impossible to get a word, so I forced my way from the throng, feeling more respect for Mrs Jacoby and more pity for Maria who, each night, whether in London, Paris, Rome or Vienna, must have to face first the demands of performance and then the demands of her admirers.

I left by the stage door and entered the alley beside the wall of the theatre, which was blocked at its end by a high wall. As I left the door and was turning to

walk towards the street, I observed from the corner of
my eye a movement in the darkness at the far end of
the alley, by the wall, some ten or twelve feet away
from me. Suddenly a hulking figure rose up from the
ground where evidently it had been crouching. The man
was enormous, almost a giant, clad in some long dark
coat. All I could see was the whiteness of a face and long,
unkempt, dark hair. I stared, appalled and expecting a
plea for money or an attack, but neither came. The
man, who had inclined his head towards me almost
as if studying me, then once more sank slowly to the
ground, again becoming invisible, part of the darkness.
Having feared attack, I now conceived of some sick and
starving wretch, too weak to beg, seeking only a quiet
place to sleep. I found a coin in my pocket and flung
it towards him. There was a scrabbling at the alley's
end and a growling mumble, which might have been
thanks.

I found a conveyance for hire and asked to be taken
to Victor's house in Cheyne Walk. I wanted to get this
business behind me and it was still early enough to find
the household awake.

It was on the way here that I began wondering if,
by some curious coincidence, that sad, huge figure in
the alley was the same man I had seen on the quay in
Chelsea. There could surely not be two such monstrous
figures in London. But if it had been the same man, this
time he had seemed less intimidating, more pitiable. My
main thoughts, however, were of my visit. I was anxious
to get to Victor's house before he and Elizabeth retired,
yet dreaded the conversation which would ensue after
I reproached him with his conduct towards his wife.

Men do not like to charge others in this way, knowing most have been tempted to make curs of themselves over women, and a good many have fallen.

At Cheyne Walk I heard Elizabeth Frankenstein had retired and Victor was at his club. I had kept the carriage waiting so it was to this club, the Chesterfield in Dover Street, that I now went, feeling by this time quite fatigued. Indeed, I had been half-minded to go home to bed on finding Victor out, but there was something in the face of Victor's manservant when he opened up to me and told me his master was away at his club that silently appealed to me to concern myself in this matter. Servants know all that passes in a household and this man I swear, was telling me, silently, that something was amiss at Cheyne Walk. At any rate, he seemed relieved when I had told him I would go and find his master at his club.

It was past ten when I descended into Dover Street. Few were abroad. I walked past the linkmen on the steps and entered the club's dignified portals. The club's porter was sitting in his wooden box in the hall. He directed me to the library where, he said, I would find Victor. I walked through some cold, marble-floored passageways and entered the dark, vaulted room which was the club's library. A few candles in the sconces burned here and there but the room was largely dark, book-lined walls making it seem even more sombre. Victor was alone in the room, hunched over the fire like a man who would never get warm. Even as I walked up to him I could see a change. Never a fat man, he had become thinner. His nose stood out between more emphatic cheekbones, his eyes were sunken. Far from the flamboyant adulterer

I had somehow expected, here was a wretched figure hiding away from home, but with nowhere else to go.

'Jonathan,' he said flatly, in greeting.

There was no way of presenting my mission as a cheerful visit. I looked at him as grimly as I could and said, 'I have just been at the theatre, Victor.'

'Did you see Maria?' he asked me, too quickly.

'I saw her but we did not speak. She was surrounded by a crowd. Victor – ' I appealed.

He said dully, 'You come as a missionary, I know. I will spare you the embarrassment you anticipate. Hugo Feltham is not a man to go behind another's back. He wrote to me saying that during her visit to Old Hall Elizabeth confided her anxieties about me to his wife and that he had written you a letter appealing to you to visit me and discuss the state of affairs. So let me be plain. It pains me to say this but say it I must. I love Maria Clementi. That love torments me for she does not love me in return. I am completely wretched, made all the more so because I know my good wife, who has never injured me in any way, is wretched also. I cannot sleep. I cannot work. I can think of nothing but Maria. I do not know what to do for I must have her but she will not have me.

'Do you know, Jonathan, what my plan was for this evening? Because she has forbidden me, through Mrs Jacoby, to visit the theatre every night, I was intending to go to her house, to hide in the trees of the square, to watch her arrive home in her carriage and spy out who might be with her. Then I would keep vigil opposite the house, watch the lights being extinguished and so stay on until at last I was weary enough to return here to sleep for a few hours. That is how I planned to spend this evening, Jonathan, as I did last night and will no doubt do tomorrow. You see to what state I am reduced.'

'My dear Victor!' I exclaimed.

'Do not pity me,' he said, 'for I am being punished.'

I put a log on the fire and tried to kick it into a blaze. 'Punished? Victor! For what do you think you are being punished?' The fire threw out smoke, but no flames.

'I cannot tell you that,' he said.

I suppose when I undertook to speak to Victor I had imagined that familiar kind of conversation in which a friend appeals to the husband on behalf of his distressed wife and is told either to go away and mind his own business or receives assurances, true or false, from the culprit that he plans to give up his mistress. I had not bargained for this – and, dishonourably, my heart soared. I knew I could not have Maria – or thought I could – I might – I did not know what I thought. My animal nature, where reason does not prevail, was organising my thoughts, or failing to do so. All I knew was that Victor had not possessed that wonderful creature, Maria. And that made me rejoice. If I could not have her, it would still have upset me if Victor had. In this respect I was a madman and I confess it. Those who never looked into the deep, grey eyes of Maria Clementi, never saw her dance or heard that thrilling voice may condemn me; no man who did could fail to understand what I felt.

But, meanwhile Victor had spoken of punishment, his punishment. 'What can you mean? Do you mean Maria will never love you?'

He did not reply. I continued to tussle with him as he sat there, thin and weary, seeming like a beaten man.

'My dear friend,' I said, 'it is dreadful to see you in this state. Should you not battle with this desire for Maria, which may lose you everything you hold most dear, the affections of your wife, your work – would it not be better to take your family away from London, settle for a time elsewhere, try to shake off this passion, starve it by taking it far from its object? Dishonour can only come of this. Even if Maria loved you in return, what good could you do her? She is a young woman of good reputation in a profession where few others like her are to be found. As yet there is no scandal attached to her name. Do you, a married man, truly wish to seduce her and ruin her, setting her inevitably on the path downwards?'

'Unhappily, it is a bitter truth, one I would rather not admit, but that is exactly what I wish to do. I have no care for consequences, for her or for myself. I want her to be mine.'

'You know you can only harm her, and yourself and your wife. You must summon up your will – and go away.'

'It is a punishment,' he said again.

I stared at Victor Frankenstein, that man of intellect and command.

'You think me mad,' he went on, 'but if you knew – if you only knew – if I could tell you. I am miserable and I deserve my misery.'

'Are you sure you are not answering to some fierce Calvinist God of your youth, some God of predestination, hell fire and damnation?' I appealed to him.

'You have not slept, you say, and plan some vigil in Russell Square tonight. Let me take you home – or let us even order two beds here at the club, obtain a sleeping draught for you from the porter. I will stay with you until you sleep. By morning, when you have rested, matters may look different and we can talk again. If you agree, I will send a message to Elizabeth saying where you are.'

'My presence is an affliction to my wife,' he said.

'Your absence is also an affliction to her,' I returned. 'Elizabeth loves you dearly. Come, Victor, you must go home. Let me come with you.'

He said sadly, 'What a villain, what a slave I am. How I wish my wife did not love me. How I wish Maria did.' Then he looked at me impatiently, saying, 'Jonathan – leave me. You cannot help me.'

'I cannot abandon you in this condition,' I said and, hooking my arm under his, I raised him to his feet. 'I shall take you home, see you swallow some opiate to make you sleep and return in the morning so that we can speak more of this.'

He agreed, being perhaps too weak to resist, but gazed at me as if he knew how little my plain man's approach would help his situation. Then began the dreadful nightmare ... The club's porter sent for a carriage which could not be found quickly. We stood outside, snow falling, waiting while Victor spoke disjointedly of Maria. Eventually the servant returned through the snow walking beside an aged carriage drawn by a tired horse. The journey took place with a hideous slowness as I sat wearily in the carriage, Victor beside me, staring hollow-eyed, at something I could not see.

At Cheyne Walk there was a crowd milling about outside the house. The front door stood wide open. The windows of the house were all lighted.

Victor cried out, 'My God! What is this? What has happened?' and threw himself from the carriage and ran to his house. I came rapidly behind, pushing through the people in front of the house, taking the steps two at a time, passing two maidservants clinging to each other in the doorway. By the time I reached the hall Victor had run upstairs.

The head manservant came up to me. 'What's occurred?' I asked him.

He told me the awful news. 'Mrs Frankenstein is dead. She and the little boy have been murdered. They are in her bed, both of them, with their throats cut. Both,' he said, his voice trembling, 'lying there in sheets all drenched with their blood – '

'But who –?' I asked.

'We do not know. A maid woke after the household had gone to bed, thinking she heard the sound of glass breaking downstairs. She roused me and another manservant. We lit candles and went downstairs. There we found the window of the long drawing-room, the salon, broken. It was plain an intruder had entered – '

'And Mrs Frankenstein – the boy?'

'As we blundered about downstairs in the darkness we heard a scream. Another maid, searching about upstairs had opened the door of her room and found her there, with the boy.'

I ran upstairs. I found Victor, in a room full of men staring down at the blanched face of his wife, her throat cut. The little boy, whom she had evidently taken into her bed, to comfort him, or herself, still clutched her, as if in fear. His throat also was cut.

It fell to me to drag my poor friend from the deathbed of his family, where a doctor who had been hastily summoned bent over the bodies and the smell of fresh blood filled the air. Even as I tried to get him from the room, where his wife and child lay grey and ghostly in their own blood, heavy feet overhead indicated that a search continued for the individual who had committed this atrocious crime.

It is a scene which even now I flinch to recall.

No one was found in the house, only an open attic window in the bedroom of the servant who had first been aroused by the sound of breaking glass. It was concluded that the murderer, having entered by the window of the drawing-room, had run upstairs, done his dreadful work and then, as the servants blundered about downstairs in the darkness, had run up to the attics, and made his escape from there, either clambering over the rooftops of adjacent houses or making his way perilously down the front of the house. Whatever he had done – and he was evidently a man of some speed and agility – by the time the open attic window had been discovered he was long gone; the prospect of finding him was small.

That, though, hardly concerned me, for I was with Victor, whose agony was terrible to witness. We could not use the pleasant room upstairs, made charming by his wife and so redolent of her character and taste. We were, perforce, in the very salon into which the murderer had first come. This room, created perhaps as a ballroom, was some thirty feet long and sparsely furnished. There was a sofa in front of a vast, empty grate. A spinet stood against a wall. Overhead were big chandeliers, uncandled and swathed in cloth. Because of the room's great size it was rarely used by the Frankensteins, who did not entertain on a grand scale. In this bleak apartment, snow drifting past its long windows over the darkened garden, I sat with my poor friend, able to do nothing to ease his pain. What was worse, perhaps, than the grief he felt for his wife and child were the torments of inexplicable remorse he suffered. 'My fault – my fault. Oh, my poor Elizabeth, my little child, what have I done to you?' he repeated over and over again. He sat on the floor, his head buried in the upholstery of a long, armless sofa.

As I busied myself with lighting a fire, I heard him moan, 'Better to have ended it then – when my crime was fresh.' At first I thought these agonies of guilt were caused by his having been away from the house at the time of the murder – at his club – unable to bear returning home to his wife under the burden of his love for Maria.

A normal man in such a dreadful situation might well have reproached himself in that way. Yet he did not directly accuse himself of having been absent when his wife and child died, nor did he speak of finding out and punishing the man who had done this deed. His agony seemed connected with some guilt he could not name, with a punishment he had earned but which had been visited, instead, on Elizabeth and his son.

I did what little I could to comfort him and form a buttress between him and those who came to discuss the crime, ask if he had any enemies, establish if there had been robbery, as well as murder, done in the house.

As dawn came I was at the drawing-room window while Victor lay on the couch, his despairing countenance down which tears continually poured turned to the ceiling. Glancing out, I thought I saw a figure in the trees beyond the lawn. There was little light and some mist about the dark trunks of the trees, so it was difficult to see the huge form of a man among the tree trunks, especially as he stood so still. I closed my eyes and opened them again. I still believed what I saw there was a man – and not just a man but that ogreish figure I had seen earlier outside the theatre.

'My God, Victor!' I cried out. 'I believe he is there, among the trees – the murderer!'

Victor jumped up and came towards me. I turned, left the room, ran down a passageway and pulled back the bolts of the door leading to the garden. But by the time I had got them undrawn and hastened outside there was no sign of the figure I thought I had seen. I ran across the snow – sprinkled lawn to the trees but no one was there. If he had been there, and I was still not quite sure of what I had seen, then he had escaped over the garden wall, where I found the bent-back branches of an elder bush growing close to some old crates piled up against the wall, which might have assisted him in scrambling over. I thought I saw his footprints on the path leading to the wall, but in the dim light with snow falling, then melting on the earth of the path the marks were hard to read.

I went slowly back to the house, thinking of that great, limping figure I had now seen, I thought, three times. Or had the figure been on this occasion the product of my imagination, worked on by fatigue and emotion? But if it was that same hideous creature I had seen before, was he the author of this dreadful crime? When I re-entered the drawing-room Victor was still by the window, ashen and hopeless. The early light showed deep lines carved on his face, lines which had not been there the evening before. He seemed twenty years older.

'I thought I saw a hulking brute out there.' I told him. 'I may have been mistaken. At any rate, if he was there before, he is gone now.'

Victor shivered. I took him to the fire and put a rug over his shoulders. As I did so I said, 'It may be imagination, but I believe I am haunted by a vast and ugly individual. I saw him once two months ago, by the river near this house, then last night, outside the theatre.' As I described my encounters with the man and his appearance Victor's eyes seemed to sink deeper into their sockets and he entered a state of profound and deadening despair. Then he said in a low voice, 'Then he is back.'

'You know him?' I said, startled. 'Who is he?'

Victor stood, went to the window again.

'Who?' I asked. 'Who, Victor? Who is this enemy?' For I assumed this man and the murderer were one and the same.

Victor turned to me and through the half-dark of the room said, 'Do not ask who, Jonathan. Ask rather what – what fiend – what thing – is that?' And then merciful nature came to his rescue and he fainted.

SEVEN

V ictor lay ill for many days. I insisted I must summon his parents from Switzerland, but this he would not allow. When I pressed him to ask them to come, he became agitated, so I assumed temporary responsibility for his health for a time. My first thought was to persuade him to leave that house in which his wife and child had been slain. I even wondered if the murderer would return to strike again, for it was very obscure what the man's motive had been in killing an innocent woman and child, and I had become doubtful whether the matter could be as simple as a thief interrupted and killing those who might identify him. Victor, though, refused to remove to Mrs Downey's, who had sympathetically agreed to assist a man she did not know. He was so insistent about staying where he was that I yielded, thinking more argument would impede his recovery and instead hired, as well as nurses for Victor, two sturdy watchmen to protect him.

For the first week he lay in a raging fever, but later improved, at which point I felt it safe to ask him who he thought the man in the garden might have been and whether he thought he had any part in the murders. But he only replied, 'I cannot tell you. To tell you anything would mean telling you everything and that I cannot do – cannot.' And with that he turned his wasted face from me on the pillow.

'Victor,' I persisted, 'tell me, I implore you. Describe the man. Say what he is to you.'

He turned a tear-stained face to me and whispered, 'Jonathan – please leave me.' And I was forced to go, though I could not believe that with such a weight as seemed to be pressing on his mind, my friend's recovery could be either quick or complete.

Meanwhile, Hugo and Lucy Feltham, who had heard of the death of Elizabeth Frankenstein and her son, arrived in London to stay with Victor and do what they could for him. Slowly he recovered his health.

EIGHT

It was at this time that Mrs Downey's sister Mrs Alice Frazer arrived from Scotland. Mrs Frazer did not generally travel with her husband since they had one of those comfortable marriages whose happiness depends to some extent on the couple spending considerable portions of their time apart. Therefore she always brought with her on the long journey south a stout young man, twenty years of age, Donald Gilmore by name, who protected her while travelling and accompanied her about London when she wished to go out alone. However, once in town there was little for Gilmore to do, so the custom was that, since he was a skilful man especially as regards carpentry, Mrs Downey would set him to repairing her house where repairs were needed.

Some two weeks after the murders, an afternoon was dictated by Mrs Feltham to be Victor's first excursion into the outside world since his illness. Therefore a party consisting of Victor and Hugo and Lucy Feltham arrived at the front door in Gray's Inn Road. Young Gilmore was at the open door, in the act of filing off the bottom, for it had begun to stick. I had just gone out into the hall to look into the street to see if the guests were arriving when their carriage drew up. I therefore saw all that happened as they descended. Victor, well muffled up and appearing still very weak, began to walk to the door leaning on Hugo's arm. It was then that Gilmore, seeing three people intending to enter the house, straightened up and stood beside the door to allow them through. As they walked past him into the hall Gilmore glanced at Victor, whose scarf was half pulled up over his face, then peered at him searching. To the astonishment of all of us, he cried out harshly, 'Frankenstein!' and raced in a state of obvious fear down the steps of the house and out into the street. I heard him cry out again from the street, as he went running off, 'Frankenstein!'

Mrs Downey, who had come to the parlour door to greet the guests, asked in a bewildered manner, 'What was that? Where is Gilmore?' But none of us, of course, could tell her. I shut the front door and we went into the parlour for tea. Once Victor was settled in front of the parlour fire she asked him how he came to know the man, Mrs Frazer's servant, but Victor professed as much bewilderment as the rest of us and said that, inasmuch as he had observed the man in the doorway, whom he had taken to be a carpenter employed from outside the household, he had no idea who he was.

'A mystery indeed,' Mrs Downey remarked, pouring the tea.

'Yet he knew your name, Victor. Is that not curious?' Lucy Feltham persisted, but Mrs Downey, seeing her guest to be uncomfortable and knowing him to be barely recovered from a serious illness, capably turned the conversation in other directions and under her agreeable guidance the short visit passed off well. Victor, though subdued, seemed in a little better spirits. Later we prevailed on Mrs Downey, who played and sang charmingly, to entertain us all.

Nevertheless, after our guests had taken themselves off, Mrs Downey, having ascertained from the maid that Gilmore had not returned, looked at me gravely and began to speculate about why he had run away. 'My sister will be most upset if he does not come back,' she said, 'for he has been with her since boyhood. His father, an Orkney boatman, was drowned at sea when Donald was twelve years old and as his mother was also dead the village sent him off to his only surviving relative, my sister's butler. Mrs Frazer found some work for him, helped, I believe, with his education, which was utterly lacking when he came, and he has been with the household ever since.' And then each of us repeated the same thing to each other several times – I, 'How can it be that this young man who spent most of his time in the wilds of Scotland, could have come across Victor Frankenstein?' and she, 'Young Donald is the steadiest fellow in the world. What can have prompted such behaviour?'

When Mrs Frazer returned she was very astonished and put out by Gilmore's disappearance. She could not account for her servant's recognising Victor, or understand why the sight of him could have caused

him such fear. Next day, we concluded, if the man
had not returned we must try to find him, but when
we retired that night Gilmore had still not come back
to the house.

However, the following morning at breakfast a maid
reported she had earlier let the shivering Gilmore in,
though, she added, he had not been prepared to enter
the house until she had assured him that the man he
called 'the doctor' was not inside. 'I would rather walk
back to Scotland,' he had said.

I suggested we have the man up and ask him together
what all this was about. Poor Gilmore, summoned,
came into the room twisting his hat in his hands. He
was a short, stalwart, red-haired young man, ordinarily
cheerful and good-humoured, but less so now.

Mrs Frazer opened the proceedings by telling him
roundly he had behaved very badly in running off
without permission and staying out all night. She told
him she knew him to be a most reliable and honest
young man but did not understand what had come into
him. She could not have him running the city streets
at night and very much required an explanation. He
replied without confidence, but respectfully, that she
must forgive him – he could not give her the explanation
she desired.

Mrs Frazer's colour rose. She had, she said, requested
an explanation, now she demanded one. Gilmore looked
at the carpet and then met her eyes, 'Madam – I
cannot.'

Stirrups and reins were rapidly being lost. I saw
Gilmore's dismissal by an angry mistress looming when
he looked towards me and appealed, 'Sir, – it is a

dreadful story unfit for the ears of ladies. This is why I cannot speak. It is a horrid tale I have not told before, not even to my uncle and aunt, for they would be very grieved to hear it.'

The ladies, Mrs Downey and Mrs Frazer, looked demanding and demure all at once, as ladies will when told a subject is not fit for their ears. Mrs Frazer then said that however unsuitable Gilmore's story might be, as his mistress she had a right to hear it, for unless she did, how could she judge if he was still fit for her service? She declared she was not prepared, when she left London, to find herself embarked on a long journey back to Scotland with a henchman who might take it into his head to run off at any moment. Distressed, he protested he would never do any such thing.

To cut all this short, I suggested I would take Gilmore off to a quiet spot, examine him and his reasons for disappearing and then tell his mistress only what it seemed suitable for her to hear. This proposition was icily agreed to by Mrs Frazer and her sister. Under their reproachful eyes Gilmore and I left the room and repaired to a nearby inn. There I ordered him a pint of ale, and as soon as our tankards were brought and we were settled at a table near the fire I asked him to explain himself.

With his honest eyes on me, speaking in the soft tones of the Orkneys – and speaking well, for he was an intelligent young man – he told me a story to upset all my previous notions of Victor Frankenstein – a dreadful story.

NINE

We were alone in the tavern as Gilmore began his tale. He said, 'I met the doctor, Frankenstein, before I came to the mainland, when I was a boy living with my father in the Orkneys. My mother was dead, having lost her life in bearing me. It was a poor life. Our bleak little hamlet on the coast was connected to the main island by a causeway which was uncovered by the tide only twice a day. It was a very hard life. We were no more than ten families and even then the sea and the land could barely keep us. We lived mainly by fishing in our rough seas; the land was not fertile. It was riches among us to have a full set of saucepans, sufficient bedding to keep us warm at night; luxury to have enough fuel in winter and enough to eat. I tell you of our poverty and the uncertainty of our lives to explain – excuse – the work my father did later – for Dr Frankenstein.'

'Frankenstein came to the island?' I asked.

'He lived there.' Gilmore told me. 'He came one day with wagons and took over a large, empty house on the hill above the village. This had in olden times belonged to a smuggler who had made his living through contraband and robbing wrecks – sometimes wrecking ships himself for his own gain. But he had been caught and hanged some years before and a stop put to him and to that trade. Dr Frankenstein brought with him three sturdy henchmen who did all the work of the place. So – he moved into the house.'

Gilmore paused, wrestling with his feelings and finally said, 'My father was not a gentle man, nor a clever one, but he loved me and was anxious for me, motherless as I was, with only one other living relative in the world, my uncle, and he a man neither of us had seen or heard from for many years. My poor father feared what would become of me if he were to die at sea while I was still young. So he became fixed on money, saved every penny he could of the little we got. His idea was to get somewhere else, perhaps even as far as America, where there was an opportunity to escape the trap of poverty and hardship in which we were caught.

'Then the doctor moved in and father began to work for him in ways he should not. This is why I have never even spoken to my uncle of this, for he would be distressed if he knew what my father had done – and what, I regret, I did to help him. And for many years I was afraid of the law, though now I am older I do not think they would be hard on a man like me who did what he should not when a boy under his father's orders. But as a lad I would lie awake at night, dwelling on what had happened over in Orkney.

It was like a nightmare but true and far worse than any dream.'

Here Donald Gilmore was again silent. 'I believe I shall shed some of my burden by telling you what occurred.'

And I nodded and agreed, little guessing how heavy a load would fall on my own shoulders with the easing of Donald Gilmore's burden. But even at that moment I suspected that what I was to hear about Victor Frankenstein, whom I so much liked and admired, would reflect badly on him. But to deny knowledge, I then thought, was almost to deny God himself. I am less sure of this now. So I said, 'Well, Donald, my good fellow, I am sure whatever you did was done in youth and ignorance. So continue your story.'

'You must imagine, Mr Goodall,' said he, 'the effect it had on us, living on our poor, wild coast with the land so sparsely covered with soil we were hard put to get any crops from it, when from Lerwick one day, going through the single street of our village, came laden wagons making their difficult way up the hill to where the old unoccupied house of the smuggler stood. This was a low stone house on a cliff with some dignity to it. The main windows faced out to sea. There was a forecourt in a paved yard and on either side of this there were big stone buildings, one a barn, one stables with enough stalls for several horses. Both house and outbuildings were dilapidated. Without more ado the doctor began to repair them, paying some attention to the barn and part of the stables, for he let it be known he was a scientist, on the island to get enough peace for his work, and these were to be his laboratories.

'This meant little to us. We were pleased enough to get work from him, the men to build, the women to clean and prepare the house. We looked forward to more work and more pay from that quarter, but as soon as the house was ready Dr Frankenstein made it very plain that he had no more use for us and moreover he had his three burly men keep watch over his premises, day and night. They would accost any man or woman who came up to the house and ask them what they wanted, telling them they had no need to call on the doctor for anything and generally seeing them off. And from that moment on we saw little of Dr Frankenstein, only his horse going through the street. So the goodwill which existed earlier for the doctor began to evaporate. Rumours started up – that he was practising black arts, that in his converted stable he was keeping some kind of strange animal which was never seen. And truly, strange noises came to us in the village, when the wind was right, noises the like of which we had never heard before. Being ignorant people, we told each other the animal must be a lion, a tiger or a bear and only felt very deprived that he would not let us come to the house to see it.

'Then, alas, our troubles began. Dr Frankenstein, during the repairing and preparation of his house, had often made use of my father's sturdy little boat to fetch and carry from the mainland, and now he asked him if he would take the boat to the Low Countries to collect an item of which he must never speak. He would be well paid for this. My father agreed and I went along with him to lend a hand with the sails, as this was to be a long journey for such a small craft and apart from my father and myself, only the doctor and two of his men were to go. Frankenstein's other men was left behind to guard the house.

'We made our voyage successfully, landing at Ostend where we took on board some crates, the largest by far having been conveyed earlier by boat from Dieppe, and being labelled "Paris". This measured some ten feet by eight and appeared, from the weight and the sound which came from inside, to contain liquid, for the sound of it slopping about was audible. Indeed, it was so heavy that at Ostend we had to get it aboard with a winch – this alarmed the doctor who knew that there was no such equipment to be had at our harbour in the Orkneys. Two days later we were back and unloading. The largest crate, that which contained the liquid, was hauled off and put on a waiting wagon with the improvised assistance of the ropes and pulleys we used to haul our boats up the beach. The wagons then set off slowly up the hill to the doctor's isolated house, but on account of the weight of the largest box and the general difficulties of unloading, Dr Frankenstein asked my father to come along to help. My father dispatched me to a neighbour's. Thus the party set off, one of the men in front with a lantern, for it was late, the other driving the wagon with the doctor and my father walking behind to relieve the weight. Now – though my father had sent me to a neighbour – I did not go. Instead, I followed on and thereby saw my father's guilt.'

'You cannot blame him for accepting a desperately needed commission to take a boat to the Continent –' I began.

'Not that – no,' Gilmore assured me. 'It was because of the large box – or rather, what was in it.' He paused. His honest face had been grave throughout his whole recital and now took on an expression of misery. 'Imagine me, a boy who had never been away from Orkney,' he said sadly, 'I had seldom been even as far as Lerwick, suddenly transported to the Low Countries in the company of such a man as the doctor, so different from us fisherfolk that he might have come from off the moon – then sent back on the instant to stop in a dark cottage with a tallow candle burning. I followed on secretly, curious to see what would happen, taking a sheep path which ran from above the village right along to where, on a ledge, I could look down on the house of the doctor from about twenty feet above. If it had been daylight, and the men less occupied with getting their heavy freight uphill without toppling over the wagon, I would have been spotted for sure. As it was, some time before they entered the courtyard I was safe in my eyrie, peering down. It took some courage, though, to stay in my position for down below was the grange in which Frankenstein kept his animal, whatever it was, and it was groaning fit to bust, poor creature – whether the men left behind had maltreated it or whether it had some affection for its master and knew him to be coming I do not know. But it groaned and moaned in a blood-chilling way, and it was dark and the surf crashed on to the shore below the house – only curiosity conquering cowardice kept me in place that night.

'Then the wagons reached the top of the hill and turned on to the paved area before the house. The unloading of the boxes began, the men, including my father, taking the cargo from the wagon either into the outbuilding opposite where I was, which I knew to be the doctor's laboratory, or into the house. A man had brought a torch and set it in the entrance of the house, and Frankenstein held aloft a lantern.

'Meanwhile the groaning of the beast in the old barn became louder and more pitiful. It began to bang itself against the door holding it in, but the men took no notice. They had left the off-loading of the largest crate until last, for that would be the most difficult task. Then, with two men on the wagon, one of them my father, and two more below, they eased the large crate to the back of the cart, the doctor nearby holding up the lantern. The plan was evidently to push the big crate forward until one end was supported by the two men on the ground, while the weight at the back end would be taken by the men on the wagon. Thus they would ease it off gradually. But it was not to be. The two on the ground had just begun to edge the rear end of the crate forward from the wagon when the beast, whose complaints had subsided to a sort of rumble, suddenly gave out a huge, echoing scream. It began to batter furiously at the door of its prison. The shock of this noise – for later we found it had been loud enough to be heard as far away as the village below – caused someone to falter in the difficult business of getting the crate from the wagon. It fell, the men leapt clear – it broke open.

And there, lying half in, half out of a vast, spreading pool of liquid, was the naked body of a young woman, her golden hair spread all about her. I suppose she had been lying in that fluid all the while.'

'Dead?' I asked.

'I thought so then,' he said. 'I thought it was a corpse.'

'She was alive?' I questioned, amazed.

'Yes,' he said gravely, 'alive!' He went on, 'She was motionless, lying, so white in that puddle, with all her long hair seeming to be floating round her. I still recall it, as if it were before my eyes. I had never seen a naked woman before,' he told me.

'A most terrifying way to encounter one for the first time,' said I, attempting to disguise my consternation. I wondered if this spectacle, seen in semi-darkness by a mere boy, had been exactly what he supposed it to be. Surely that had not been the figure of a real woman? Had it not been a model or perhaps some rare kind of ape with an uncanny resemblance to the human? Easier to think those thoughts, rather than that Victor Frankenstein had imported a woman, dead or alive, in order to conduct some experiments upon her. 'What happened then?' I demanded.

'The doctor was greatly concerned, exclaimed aloud and cursed the men for their clumsiness as he tenderly gathered up the woman and carried her in his arms, her long hair drooping down over his arm, into the house. And all this time the creature in the barn kept roaring and, as soon as I had got over the shock of seeing the crate fall and the woman lying there, I took to my heels and raced back to where I was meant to be, hoping my father would never find out about my hiding on the hill that night, as he did not.'

'He never spoke to you of this?'

'Never. Though he may have spoken to others, for I know it was later said, behind men's hands, that Dr Frankenstein had imported a woman, drugged, to

Orkney for his use. He was rich; we were poor and afraid. Nothing was done.'

'Unlike what we hear of the stout-hearted Orkneyman,' said I.

'Stout hearts sink when bellies are empty,' Gilmore replied. 'The men feared that if they reported the doctor for kidnapping or the like, the law would be turned against them and they would be taken away from hungry wives and children.'

I shook my head, 'This story of a woman drugged and brought to Orkney by Frankenstein seems to me most unlikely, Gilmore, from everything I know of the man.'

'I cannot help that, sir,' he responded doggedly. 'I am telling you the truth – and the truth gets worse. For after this we did not see the woman again, though my father was again employed by the doctor, this time to take a crate, much the same as the last, to Dublin. But there was no liquid inside it. The crate was landed at Dublin, where the doctor stayed for a week. Then he came back with my father in the ship, but this time without the crate.'

I looked sharply into Gilmore's eyes, searching for the truth. Either the man was a consummate liar who actually believed his own lies, or he was telling the truth as he knew it. 'You think he took the woman to Dublin in a crate?' I asked, incredulously. 'Left her there and came back alone?'

'But it was not the woman,' he said, 'for we saw her at his house, while the doctor was away.'

'Saw her?' I repeated, astonished.

'That is how I know she was alive. For she was in

the house while the doctor and my father were away on their voyage. The doctor had left only one of his guards behind and once he was gone this man, a big fellow, speaking a harsh tongue none could understand, seized the opportunity to come down to the village and drink and try to get hold of a woman. So I and another lad, knowing there was no one at the house, ran up the hill to see what we could spy out and there she was. We peeped through a big window on the ground floor and there was the young lady, in a blue dress, lying asleep on a couch, with a kind of picture book, like one for a child, in her hand, and all her long fair hair trailing over the sofa. She was, indeed, a lovely sight,' Gilmore said. 'So young and so pretty, with a sort of innocence on her sleeping face.'

'Not dead?' I asked.

'No, not dead; for we saw her stir a little as we watched – and we, fearing she would wake and spot us, ran off laughing, like the two young loons we were. But we never saw her again. Thereafter the house stayed guarded. Rumours grew; there was more bad feeling against the doctor, and my father too, for helping him. I do not know how it would have ended, but not two weeks after the doctor and my father came back from Ireland we awoke to the sound of the doctor's wagon going hell for leather through the village street, heading for the causeway. His men carried flares, all his baggage was piled up behind – and even as they left the village we saw the flames of a great fire on the hill. The doctor's house burned down – not entirely, of course, for it was solid stone, but enough to destroy anything in the buildings and most of the timber as well, bringing in the roofs. We thought he must have started the fire himself, for all his possessions had been packed up and loaded, we supposed, before the fire began. The wagons were out of the village almost before we knew it, so we did not know if the doctor himself, or all his men, or the pretty woman, survived the fire.'

Gilmore paused. 'So now, sir, you will understand, perhaps, why seeing the man you call Mr Victor Frankenstein made me run for my life. For I truly believe,' he said in a low voice, 'that he, Frankenstein, is the Devil, or something very near it.'

Still between doubt and belief, I again studied Gilmore's face, searching it as if it could provide the answer to my questions. How could Victor – that frank, honest, open, studious, serious man – a man of whom it was impossible to think badly – how could he have hidden himself away in Orkney to indulge in such mysterious and seemingly evil practices as Gilmore spoke of? Yet it could not be denied that Gilmore had instantly recognised Victor as he came through the door at the house in Gray's Inn Road or that the sight had plainly terrified him. Small wonder, if there was any truth in his tale. Was it possible Gilmore had been traduced into inventing this story? But what possible reason would anyone have to bribe him to say such things? The only way to explain Gilmore's story without believing Victor to be a villain, or practitioner of the black arts, was to conclude that Gilmore, a mere boy at the time, with no wide experience of the world, had misunderstood what had happened on Orkney.

What he said next did little to support this theory. 'I do not now believe it was a beast he had penned up in the barn,' he said slowly. 'I thought it was then, but now I believe it was a man, some suffering idiot crying out in pain and incomprehension. But what would he have been doing to the poor creature, all that while?'

I confessed to him that the same thought had occurred to me as he told his story. What I did not tell him was that what had crossed my mind, as he spoke, was a vision of that hideous creature I had seen at the dock, outside the theatre and in the trees at the end of Victor's garden after poor Elizabeth's murder. If Gilmore's report were correct in its essentials, then was it such a flight of fancy to imagine that whatever unfortunate creature Victor had kept in captivity had returned in order to take a hideous revenge? That would explain Victor's passivity in the face of his wife's murder and his belief that somehow he himself was the cause of the calamity.

And yet – we know man can be boundlessly cruel, that some evil men take pleasure in the torment and suffering they cause to others. But how could I believe Victor Frankenstein one of those men, one who would capture and torment a fellow creature – or seize a woman and take her helpless to a remote island to enjoy her? I could not believe it; the thought was impossible.

Gilmore regarded me sympathetically. 'I am sorry to be bearer of this ill news concerning your friend, sir. I assure you all I have said is true to the best of my knowledge.'

'I am sure that is so, Gilmore,' I said, 'but we must think of the present now. I will tell Mrs Frazer something of this story – enough, I hope, to satisfy her and persuade her to keep you on.'

As we walked back I became suddenly alarmed. If

there were any chance that Victor was being trailed by a madman, then the man might have tracked him to Mrs Downey's on the afternoon he visited us. This could put the household at risk. If the madman had killed Elizabeth Frankenstein (who had not even known her husband at the time Gilmore described) then he might just as easily, in his insanity, take his revenge on others connected with Victor.

On the way back to the house I therefore said to Gilmore, 'I am still confused by your story, but I am greatly afraid that Mr Frankenstein may be being pursued by someone who wishes to hurt him or those who know him. Mrs Frankenstein is already dead, murdered. And at Mrs Downey's house there are, at present, two ladies, a child and female servants. All may be in danger. Whatever the truth of your story, Gilmore, you must promise me that you will never in any circumstances go off as you did before. There must be a strong and active man in the house at all times.'

Gilmore frowned and asked, 'Who is the doctor's enemy, do you think?'

'I am sure of nothing,' I told him, 'but I think it possible he is that unfortunate creature Mr Frankenstein kept in captivity on Orkney. We must take precautions for a while. You had better say nothing of this to the household. You must be vigilant, but keep the reasons for your vigilance secret.'

He nodded in agreement. As we hurried back to Gray's Inn Road I thought of Hugo and Lucy Feltham, and how they were, in all innocence, bearing the grieving Victor company at Cheyne Walk. Ought I to warn them they might be in danger? However unpleasant it might be I must now confront Victor with Gilmore's story at the earliest moment. Even Maria Clementi, outside whose theatre the creature had been waiting, might be in peril. Unhappily, I recognized I must act.

TEN

Returning to the house I explained as calmly as I could to Mrs Downey and her sister Mrs Frazer that Gilmore, as a boy, had met Victor while he was conducting experiments on Orkney. Being young and infected with the superstitious ignorance of a small and unlettered community, he had taken Victor for some kind of wizard, and conceived a great fear of him. On seeing him unexpectedly in London, that fear had suddenly revived, thus his flight. Yet, I told them, there was some evidence that during his days on the island Victor had made an enemy. Since his wife had been murdered, and the murderer was as yet uncaught, it might be wise to take precautions against anyone who might do any of us some harm. I suggested that until there was proof that my fears were unfounded, either Gilmore or I should remain in the house at all times; and that one of us should accompany the ladies on any outing or visit they might make. Other ladies might have welcomed such consideration for their safety, but these sisters, whether by reason of temperament or upbringing were not so inclined to do.

Mrs Downey and Mrs Frazer were the daughters of a lawyer, John Jessop, and had been reared in Cornwall on a small estate (so small one might call it a garden, Mrs Downey once merrily told me). Mr Jessop practised law in the nearby town. The family on both sides was well connected, but the Jessops were not rich. Mrs Jessop, being a reading woman, whom some might have termed a blue-stocking, was not the most careful mama in the world. Her two daughters spent more time with the village children, blocking up streams, stealing watercress from farmers' fields and the like, than some parents would think advisable for young ladies. Nevertheless, young ladies they were, though from an unconventional household liberal in its ways of thinking. The late Mr Downey was the son of Mr Jessop's partner. When he and the young Cordelia Jessop made a match they removed to London, where, after only eight years of marriage, Downey died, leaving his wife little more than the lease on the small house in Gray's Inn Road. Her mother's sister had mercifully left her a little money some years earlier, so she was able to continue to make a home for herself and her little girl Flora.

To make ends meet, Mrs Downey decided to take a lodger. How I became that man is easy to tell. Two years earlier I had come to London to pursue my researches. Needing a spot near to the libraries and individuals whom I should need to consult, I asked at an inn where I might find lodgings in the neighbourhood. I was directed up the street to Mrs Downey's. I was a little surprised to discover when I met my prospective landlady that the widow looking for lodgers was not a motherly woman of forty but a young woman of twenty-six. But as she appeared to have a clear sense of what she was doing in the matter of candles, laundry and chops, I took the rooms. It was not until I had been there six months that I discovered I was Mrs Downey's first lodger – I was also to be her last, but that tale comes later.

This digression may help to explain why Mrs Downey and Mrs Frazer were not happy about recommendations without explanations. Respectable as they were, they had been reared according to the advanced principles of education promulgated by Mr Godwin and French savants such as M. Jean-Jacques Rousseau. According to these men, there ought to be very little discrimination between boys and girls as far as their education and rearing is concerned. Training had produced a very curious, animated, questioning, independent spirit in Mrs Frazer and Mrs Downey. Admirable as this spirit might be in many ways, it does not produce blind obedience to male suggestions and wishes (and was, I believe, one of the chief reasons for the less than cordial relations between Mrs Frazer and her husband). Therefore I left the house as the questions began, abandoning Gilmore, I suspected, to an interrogation which would make him wish he had fallen, rather, into the hands of the Spanish Inquisition. I had to trust him not to reveal too much of his horrible and mysterious story when pressed, yet had no choice, I thought, but to leave him to his fate, for I had to speak to Victor.

I decided first, however, to visit Maria Clementi's house and communicate my suspicions of the man I had seen outside the theatre to Mrs Jacoby, asking her if she, too, had observed him on any occasion.

When I arrived, Maria was not at home. Ushered into a small sewing-room upstairs, I found myself addressing Mrs Jacoby as she bent over a heap of theatrical costumes to which she was making repairs. It was not a cordial welcome. I launched into my story, telling her bent head much of what I had told the ladies at Gray's Inn Road. I added that I had seen a hulking figure concealed outside the very theatre at which Maria was performing, and that I suspected he might be the same man I had observed in Victor's garden on the night of the murder of his wife. Victor, I said, might have an enemy in this man and since the murder of Mrs Frankenstein, it behoved all who knew him to take precautions to ensure their own safety. I was not sure how much of this strange story was believed. As I concluded she put down her work, lifted her head and told me robustly that she had already called on the services of an old sergeant of her husband for the defence of the household.

After a pause she apparently came to some resolution and, with angrily tightened lips, told me, 'There would seem to be matters connected with Mr Frankenstein of which you are unaware. My decision to employ a strong man in the house was taken for reasons not unconnected with Mr Frankenstein, but I do not want them spoken of on every corner. I would not tell you of this had you not come here with this strange story. But you have, and now I will relate what occurred here only yesterday.'

This was of course the very day when Victor had been

brought to Gray's Inn Road, and Gilmore, recognising him, had run off. Mrs Jacoby then told me that Victor, very weak, had arrived at Russell Square in the early evening accompanied by some friends who had been very reluctant to let him leave the carriage. The lady of the party, Mrs Feltham, had come to the door saying that Mr Frankenstein, who was travelling back to his home with them, had suddenly insisted on visiting Russell Square to see Maria Clementi about an urgent matter.

Plainly, Mrs Jacoby told me, she was unhappy about the proposed visit but could not prevent it. She appealed for Mrs Jacoby's cooperation in making the visit a short one for Mr Frankenstein was still weak after an illness.

Mrs Jacoby had agreed to all this, though reluctantly, but told me, 'I was very unhappy he had come. Let us be quite candid – before his wife's death Mr Frankenstein was seized with an alarming passion for Miss Clementi and I feared that, in spite of his bereavement, that emotion had returned. I believe Mrs Feltham knew this and also disapproved of the visit.

'I am employed to guard Miss Clementi against the sort of scandal which attaches itself to young women in prominent positions. I exist, moreover, to spare her agitation and fatigue. Mr Frankenstein's visit was not welcome to me.'

According to Mrs Jacoby, Lucy Feltham returned to the carriage to wait. Victor descended and entered the house looking, Mrs Jacoby said, very ill and feverish. He pleaded for an interview alone with Maria, even if it were to last only five minutes. His manner was so agitated she thought it better to agree to a brief meeting between the two in private, if this was Maria. But she herself would be in the adjoining room all the time. Her aim, she said, was to get this interview over quickly and calmly and set the sick man on his way home with his friends.

Maria agreed to see Victor alone in the small drawing-room for five minutes. Mrs Jacoby therefore retreated to the dining-room, with which it was connected by large double doors. She sat down and kept her eye fixed firmly on the clock. But not a minute after Maria entered the drawing-room she heard Victor's voice raised in passionate speech, though whether his tones were those of love or anger she could not tell. The voice went on and on and she was about to interrupt the interview, even before the agreed five minutes were over, when she heard him cry out in a dreadful voice, 'Maria! Maria! You will be the death of me!', then leave the drawing-room and, indeed, the house, slamming the front door behind him.

She had rushed into the room to find Maria, very white, collapsed in a chair and unable, of course, to give any account of what Victor had said or what he wanted. Plainly, said Mrs Jacoby, Mr Frankenstein had upset her very much – and not, she added grimly, for the first time. 'I shall not let him in the house again,' she told me. 'To do so would be insanity. He is a sick man and, I believe, deranged. I dread to think of the state of mind of a man returning to pay court to a woman two weeks – two weeks! – after the death of his wife. Yet what else could his visit have meant? If that is so, then he is a monster. The story you have just told me of an enemy keeping watch on him is unpleasant. Whether it is entirely true I do not know – but of such a man as Mr Frankenstein I must tell you I can believe almost anything. To be honest, I half-suspected when you first arrived he had persuaded you to come and press his case with Maria. I apologise for that suspicion. But now you see why I have already sent for a sturdy man to guard the door. I cannot have him here again. And if you have any sense at all, Mr Goodall, I should leave this matter strictly alone. It is none of your business and involving yourself in it can only harm you.'

I stood up. 'In spite of all, Mrs Jacoby,' I said, 'I still regard Mr Frankenstein as a friend and I am going now to speak to him and try to help him.'

'I wish you joy of it, then,' she said. 'And if you will take my advice you will get him to a quiet spot far from London where, with help, he can recover his strength and his sanity.'

As I left the door a carriage came up the street towards me. In it I saw a smiling Maria Clementi, a young woman I imagined to be her servant, and that degenerate, Gabriel Mortimer, dressed in his burgundy coat and trousers, a tall green hat on his head from which his jet ringlets hung down in profusion. He and Maria seemed to be laughing together at some remarks of his. Having no wish to encounter them when they dismounted from the carriage, I turned, as if I had not seen them, and went off rapidly in the other direction, searching for a hackney carriage to take me to Cheyne Walk.

I thought of that merry party in the carriage. How could the delicate Maria Clementi manage to stay on those terms with a fellow of such an obviously disreputable kind? What a strange household that was — in spite of an appearance of honesty, even Mrs Jacoby did not seem utterly candid and open. I could not decide whether she was what she purported to be, the loyal friend and protector of Maria, or a woman of a more sinister and self-interested kind.

On my journey to Chelsea snow began to fall. My heart sank at the prospect of the necessary but unpleasant interview I would be forced to have with Victor. Only a few weeks before I had been reproaching him with his conduct towards his wife. Now I was searching him out in order to imply there might be some unadmitted, shameful secret in his past. It would not do, I thought. I must disentangle myself from the web of Victor's affairs, part of which was the enticing, fascinating Maria.

I was pleased to hear, when I arrived, that Mrs Feltham was out, calling on friends. I wanted neither to raise spectres in front of her nor to be forced to draw Victor aside in order to speak to him.

I was shown into the study, where I found Victor in a chair by a roaring fire. A shawl was over his knees. Hugo was leaning negligently against the desk, upon which lay a half-empty bottle of claret. The two were laughing as I entered. I felt a little foolish when I saw all this. Here was I, bent on investigating a dark secret involving a friend, on warning the household of danger; there was Victor, glass in hand, health plainly much restored, enjoying a pleasant afternoon. I looked at him as he greeted me with a smile. I could not believe that this was the same man I had seen desperate for Maria Clementi, seen racked with remorse after the death of his wife and child, and who now, if Mrs Jacoby was to be believed, had resumed his courtship, with wife and child barely cold in their graves. And then, there was Gilmore's tale of what had happened in Orkney. My heart failed me. It seemed impossible Victor had anything with which to reproach himself. Yet I had come to the house for a purpose and decided, most reluctantly, to fulfil it, although knowing this interview might well cost me some part of a friendship.

Victor began by offering me wine, which I declined. I asked him where were the two men I had employed on his behalf to guard the house while the madman who had killed Elizabeth and the child was still at large, for I had seen no trace of them when I arrived. 'Oh,' Victor responded to my enquiry, 'I discharged the fellows. I did not like having them about and I have come to the conclusion, as has the magistrate, that the murderer was a thief who disturbed my wife as he went about his business and wickedly killed her to avoid detection. The magistrate thinks, and so do I, that he is unlikely to return to the scene of his crime.'

In a voice I knew to be less confident than his own, I asked, 'But what of the man I saw lurking in the trees in your garden on that dreadful night, the same man, I believe, I saw earlier in the evening outside the theatre where Miss Clementi was performing?'

'I did not see the man myself on either occasion,' replied Victor. 'And nor, I believe, did anyone else.'

'Dear God,' I burst out. 'Are you telling me I imagined that man? Victor – do not deceive yourself or your friends. There is some bad work afoot here. That young man who left my landlady's house so suddenly yesterday when you arrived was Donald Gilmore, her sister's servant, son of the boatman you employed when you were on Orkney. You did not recognise him because since you last saw him he has turned from a boy into a man. But he knew you the moment he saw your face – and named you. He has told me of the woman you caused to be brought to the island in his father's boat, of a creature you kept in the barn, of the guards around your house – of a fire. Victor – do you not think that all this had something to do with that malformed creature who appears to be watching you and those you know, and with the death of your wife and the boy? For your own safety, and ours, be frank.'

He regarded me with a steady demeanour, perfectly at ease. But I noticed his face had gone very pale.

Hugo was gazing at me in astonishment. He asked, 'Jonathan – what is all this?'

Victor only said, 'So that was Gilmore's lad. He was but a boy when I was in the Orkneys. The fisherfolk there did not like me. Indeed, they feared me. I had thought to find peace for my scientific researches in that remote spot, but in the end was driven off by hostile and superstitious local folk. I had my house guarded because I knew their temperament. I had reason to think that one night, after drink and inflamatory remarks at the bare cottage room they called the tavern, they might march on me and do me and my work harm. Indeed, I think they may have started the fire which burned my house. I do not take it at all kindly, Jonathan, that you chose to discuss me and my affairs with your landlady's sister's servant and give your attention to wild boyish tales he related to you. Now you come here fantastically prating of some imaginary enemy – '

I was shaken by his all too plausible denials. Yet there was at least one fact in a cloud of what Victor correctly pointed out to be hearsay. I cried 'You *saw* the man in your garden. His appearance distressed you. You spoke of guilt – '

'My wife had been murdered a few hours before. And my only son,' Victor said shortly. His tone was very cold.

I stood quite still, as shocked as if he had struck me. Either I was a fantasist or my friend Victor was a cold-blooded liar.

Hugo the peace-maker intervened. 'Jonathan,' he appealed, 'if there is some old story the man Gilmore has told you, can we not talk of it later? Victor has been ill, is still unwell.'

'Not too ill, it seems, to prevent him yesterday from descending from the carriage taking him home to have a noisy interview at Russell Square with Miss Clementi,' said I.

'So you have spoken about me to Miss Clementi's paid companion, as well as a manservant at the house you live in,' Victor said, his tone verging on the contemptuous. 'Well, I am grateful for the interest, Jonathan, you seem to be showing in my affairs. Would you like to discuss me with my butler now? May I introduce you to the boot-boy?' He paused, and regained control of himself. He continued in a less unfriendly voice, 'I went to see Miss Clementi to ask her to resume her lessons with me, as a favour to both of us, for I must work and occupy my mind so as not to dwell on the tragedy that has taken place. The sooner I begin, the better it will be for me. Jonathan, my dear man, can we not forget all that has been said here this afternoon? Let us put it behind us. Will you not sit down and take a glass of wine with us? We dine in an hour. Will you stay?'

The bewildered Hugo added his voice to Victor's, 'Stay, Jonathan, do. Shall we not sit down together, the four of us, you, Victor, Lucy and myself, and talk together as we have done in the past?'

But I shook my head and said in great confusion, 'No, no – I cannot. I must leave. Victor – I am truly sorry if I have said anything to upset you. I will go now. I must think.'

And I blundered from the room, as mortified as I have ever been in my life. The scene had not taken above ten minutes and yet, during it, I had angered Victor, shocked Hugo and acted, as I saw it, like a fool and a villain. Such scenes are forgiven, I knew, but never quite forgotten. I cursed myself as I walked quickly along, as if escaping from the house, although snow was swirling round me and the ground beneath my feet slippery. Then I saw, through the blowing snow, some hundred yards away, what I took to be a figure, dark against the surrounding whiteness. It was on top of the wall which surrounded Victor's garden. As I looked, it moved, heaved itself a little higher up and put one knee on top of the wall.

Then the man hurled himself over and dropped the ten feet or so to the ground below in a wild tangle of arms and legs. Once on the ground this individual instantly scrambled upright and began to run away down the road, with a curious lop-sided gait. He was huge – he was the man I had seen before, whose existence Victor had so recently denied – and he had been watching Victor's house.

I set off after him as fast as I could go, shouting, 'Stop! Stop, man! I must speak to you!' I did not reflect that there was no one about and that, if I caught up with him, an encounter might be the worse for me. He ran on, though looking over his shoulder, then put on speed, going quickly enough for a crippled man travelling over a slippery surface.

This chase, with both pursuer and pursued hampered and often sliding through a snow storm, might have struck an observer as comical. Yet we were both, I'm sure, in dead earnest – me to catch him, he to get away.

He crossed the road to the riverside. I followed. Then there was a sudden flurry of snow which went into my face, blinding me. When I brushed the snow from my eyes the man was gone – but I knew where he was. He had returned to the quay where I had first seen him. So I walked straight down to the strand, spied out the steps up to the wharf ahead of me (the tide was low) and struggled on to the quay. As my head rose up to the stone surface of the dock I saw, through the snow, first a braced pair of legs, then a trunk, and found myself facing a sturdy man with a sack over his shoulder. As he looked doubtfully at me I asked him, 'Have you seen a man with a limp?'

From his reply, 'Why would you want to know that?' I deduced that the man was here, though he was not to be seen.

'Who is he?' I asked. 'What is his name?'

He peered at me through the swirling snow. 'What's he done?' he asked.

'I don't know,' I replied. 'Who is he?'

'We calls him Oberon,' the fellow said, '– in jest, for the King of the Fairies, you know. We don't know his name. He says nothing. He's weak in the head, but he's strong in the back and does what he's told. They keep him on, paying him in scraps of food and copper coins. He sleeps in that shed over there and acts as watchman by night. But I wouldn't go over there and stir him up. He's meek as a lamb most of the time, but sometimes he'll fall into a sudden rage, and that makes him dangerous.'

'I must talk to him,' I said.

'I've told you – he's feeble-witted, you'll get nothing from him. But if you want him you'll find him in the hut. I've got to get this sack of wood back to my family.' And with that he plodded along the jetty and began to climb the steps up to the road.

In some apprehension I went to the wooden building the man had called the ogre's home and pushed open the door. The building was some ten feet square and used as a storehouse. At the back were piled crates and barrels, almost to the roof, while to the right were coils of rope, a pickaxe, an upright spar. But to the left a small corridor between stacked crates some three feet wide led to cleared space at the back, and there was what appeared to be a heap of bedding. In the dim light, I saw crouched, even cowering, rather like a child hiding in a cupboard, the vast figure of the man they called, cruelly, Oberon.

I could not at first make out his expression, but as I took, fearfully, a step into the hut I saw his teeth, bared in fear, like an ape's. I said, 'Fellow – man – whoever you are – tell me why you are spying on Victor Frankenstein.' The sound of the name made him start, which caused me to fall back a pace, thinking he meant to attack me. But then he lapsed into apathy again and his low, gruff voice started up, but he only babbled out an incomprehensible mix of sounds from which it was impossible to make out any words. Yet I thought he was trying to say something. 'Come,' I said. 'I mean you no harm – but I saw you in Mr Frankenstein's garden one night and today saw you come over his garden wall. What do you want with him? What have you done?'

I then saw him, in the dim light of that cold shed, sobbing, crying helplessly, wiping his eyes and nose on the sleeve of the black coat that he wore. Fearful as I had been of him, and still was, I felt pity too. And I thought I caught, mixed with his sobs and babblings, one word I could understand: 'Bride, bride, bride,' he seemed to be saying.

I copied this word back to him, 'Bride, you say? What bride?' The hideous thought came to me suddenly that poor Elizabeth Frankenstein's death could have come about because this deluded creature, watching her comings and goings from opposite her house, had persuaded himself that she was his – had broken in and, when she resisted him, killed her, and the child with her. This vision was most terrible to me.

And now he arose and began to shout, babbling, stumbling, yet, from the incoherent sentences I still thought I heard, 'my bride, my bride.' He took a step towards me. His eyes were very large and brown. They burned. Uncertain whether he was asking my help or menacing me, I retreated from the doorway, yet thought I was beginning to understand some of his incoherent speech.

'He – has – my – bride,' he seemed to be saying.

Unheroically, I did not stay to question him further about what he meant. The snow was still swirling down, we were alone and already what daylight there was began to wane. I decided on retreat. As I walked backwards from the hut in the direction of the road, I still spoke to him calmly, 'Who has your bride? Is that what ails you? Tell me what is your trouble.'

He came towards me, not, I think, with menace in mind but nevertheless, his great shambling figure was menacing enough. Then, haltingly, but clearly enough, he bellowed, 'Frankenstein!' and pointed again, as he had when I first saw him on the barge, throwing his arm to the left in the direction of Victor's house. And he cried again, 'Frankenstein!'. This time there was no doubt about the violence of his feelings.

At this, I confess, my nerve broke. I turned and ran along the paving of the quay, scrambled up the slippery steps to the road and, with one glance behind me at the top, to assure myself he was not coming after me, hastened homewards, sliding on the snow, now an inch deep, under my feet. Later, I again looked behind me to see if he was following. Seeing he was not, I slowed my pace and, wet and cold, continued to plod forward as fast as I could.

Yet in spite of my retreat it did not seem to me that

the poor, misshapen creature had meant me any real harm. He had done no more than chase me off and return to his lair. His pathetic babbling speech might have been more appeal than threat. And he had called out Frankenstein's name, called it out, it seemed to me, in pain and indignation. What could it mean? My head reeled, but this I knew – Victor's cold denials of any knowledge of this man must have been lies. He was no chimera, no figment of my imagination. Victor had not told me the truth. This greatly saddened me on the long, uncomfortable walk to my lodgings.

I arrived back at Gray's Inn Road in a deplorable state. Gilmore opened the door to me and was disconcerted by my appearance, but all I could say to him in the hall, as the parlour door flung open and Mrs Downey appeared with many exclamations, was. 'Be vigilant, Gilmore. Nothing is any better.'

Then came the usual kindly attentions from the two ladies of the house, the fire lit in the bedroom, the production of a steaming hipbath, fresh clothes and a seat at the parlour fire, feet boiling in a mustard bath like a piece of beef. Then came supper and a whisky toddy – for Mrs Frazer never came over the border without bringing with her several stone jars of her native brew. There was, however, a quid pro quo behind these kindly female attentions. In exchange the ladies required a fuller account of the story Gilmore had told me at the inn. Evidently their questioning had got little out of him. Nevertheless, further confused by the events of the day, I felt it better to say nothing. I wished I could, for safety's sake, have commanded the whole household to move to another place, away from these mysteries. But of course, as a mere lodger in the house I could not give orders and to have attempted persuasion would have meant telling all.

So, contributing nothing to the happiness of Mrs Downey and her sister, I claimed fatigue and went early to bed, but not before I had surreptitiously visited Gilmore in the kitchen, telling him we must keep watch that night over the house and requesting him to rouse me at eleven o'clock, so that he might go to bed while I stayed awake watching. When he looked at me in alarm I told him that I believed I had found Victor's enemy, that he was most probably a lunatic and not far off from here. 'He appears harmless, but that may not be his permanent state. We must be careful. Tomorrow I shall endeavour to make some better plan, but for tonight we must stay on guard.'

I then retired and lay down in my clothes to get some hours' rest. At eleven Gilmore duly shook me awake and, the rest of the household having gone to bed, I went downstairs. Looking from the window of my room, I saw that the trees, the yards behind the houses with their little patches of vegetables had turned white. The looming houses, most windows unlit, were black against the snow. From their crooked chimneys smoke still streamed into the dark night sky. As far as I could see not a footprint marred the whiteness behind the house in any direction. Nor was there any sound of traffic or people in the streets, as if the snow had laid a great, quiet blanket over all.

Downstairs, I listened out, occasionally rising from the parlour fire to look from windows, back and front, to see if there were anyone near the house. Alone, in the unusual silence snow brings to a city, I wondered if my precautions were needless. Had my imagination carried me into fantasy?

Suppose, I wondered, that a charge were laid of slandering Victor's good reputation. The prosecution could well make a strong case that I was mad – none but I had seen the ungainly, half-witted man I claimed was threatening Frankenstein. As for Gilmore, what lawyer could not easily discredit the unsupported word of a witness about what he believed to have occurred so long ago when he was a boy? Either Victor Frankenstein, my friend, was deceiving me or I was myself deluded, sorely mistaken about much in this affair. Such uncomfortable thoughts did not, though, overcome my fatigue and the warmth of the fire. I regret to report I fell asleep.

Alas, a flinging out of my arm jolted some knick-knack from the parlour table. I heard it, but slept on. Not so Mrs Downey, who, a woman to her fingertips, could in her sleep hear a pin drop in the cellar. I was woken by a cry from the doorway: 'Mr Goodall! What are you doing here? Why are you not in bed?'

Mrs Downey, a wrap over her shift, hair falling down her back, holding a candle in her hand, was a pretty sight, I thought, coming from sleep. She glanced about the room, taking in the fallen bibelot, happily unbroken, and then her eyes began to roam on, in search, I think, of the bottle or bottles she thought must be involved in the affair. I had already deduced the late Mr Downey had not been a temperate man. Yawning and rubbing my eyes I told her I was on watch for trouble, though not, as she had discovered, conscientious enough to carry out my self-designated duties.

She responded vehemently saying she could bear all this no longer. There were mysteries and secrets in the house, she knew I had anxieties I was not revealing to her, I was not to imagine she had not perceived Gilmore's extra vigilance or did not know I was at the back of it. She had not been told what Gilmore, her sister's own servant, had revealed to me as to his running off. Now there was danger – 'I repeat,' she said, 'I can bear this secrecy no longer. Surely I have a right to know what is happening? My sister's, my own and my defenceless child's safety appears threatened by a mystery. And,' she concluded, 'if you believe keeping secrets concerning myself and my family to be chivalrous then I have the honour to inform you it is not. It is merely folly.'

Like most men, I do not like to hear myself roundly abused by a woman on waking. I became a little angry. 'For God's sake, Cordelia, I am doing my best,' I exclaimed – this was the first time I had used her christian name and I was surprised to hear it burst from my lips.

She did not comment on this use of her name, only saying gently, 'Would it not be better to tell me what is happening?'

I sighed and leaned back, feeling very weary. 'It is very late, Cordelia.'

'That does not concern you for you are on watch,' she said pertly. 'I will make a little tea and butter some bread. We will call it an early breakfast and it will restore you.'

And this she did, rekindling the embers of the fire, suspending the brass kettle on its hook above it, taking the loaf set out for breakfast and toasting slices in front of the flames; while I, fighting sleep, wondered if I should tell her all, or any of the story. If I were wrong? Could it be right to pass off suppositions as truth, frightening a woman? Such struggles availed me nothing in the face of pretty Mrs Downey at work with a toasting-fork, her hair curling down her back. Looking as she did, she would have set a Trappist monk singing a roundelay. I asked myself were she indeed my sister, but widowed, with a child, would I have the right to keep knowledge and therefore the power of deciding her own affairs, from her?

So – warning her that the story I had to tell was unpleasant and frightening, and that she herself would have to decide how much of it to believe, I told her all, or almost all the story. Throughout my relation, which must have taken half an hour, she sat quietly looking at me with a level gaze, moving only when she stood to offer me tea or make more toast. I was ravenously hungry. I was astonished by her calm. At some points I thought it might be she could not understand what I was telling her but, no, she understood perfectly. I concluded my tale by weakly appealing to her for a judgment: 'Mrs Downey – Cordelia – tell me, do you think I am deluded, a false accuser of my friend Victor Frankenstein?'

Gravely she told me, 'I do not think you understand everything about this, Jonathan' (she used my own first name, I noticed). 'There are mysteries here. But

I am sure much of what you say is correct. Remember, I have known Donald Gilmore since he first came to my sister's house as a lad. His tale concerning Mr Frankenstein may not be accurate in every point, but not, I think, the fiction Mr Frankenstein makes it out to be.'

'Cordelia,' I said, and I may say the joy of using her name and having her use mine filled me. 'What you say relieves my mind. I feared I was mad.'

She said pensively. 'Not that, but I am afraid I think Mr Frankenstein a danger to you. And the singer, Maria Clementi – and very possibly her companion, too.'

I think I have said I thought Cordelia, as I now will call her, a little hard on Maria, whom she had never met, through jealousy, perhaps, and because she had a respectable woman's mistrust of actresses and the like. 'Miss Clementi is the purest and most innocent creature imaginable, as you would know if you met her,' said I.

'Whom you last saw in a carriage, laughing with a man you describe as one of the most degenerate creatures you ever encountered – '

I sighed. 'I know. It is a mystery. And now Hugo and Lucy Feltham are at Cheyne Walk and I know not what may be occurring there. Now I have dragged you into this affair. What can I do?'

'Wash your hands of the business now,' she told me.

'But I fear you and your household are in danger. How can I turn my back and pretend nothing is the matter?'

'Then go to the magistrate Mr Wortley in the morning and inform him you have reason to believe the man who killed Mrs Frankenstein is at the Chelsea wharf. Demand that he should be taken up and questioned,' said the lady, evidently once a keen student of her late husband, the lawyer.

'My dear Cordelia,' I said, taking her hand. 'Of all women you are the most excellent.'

She seized back her hand. 'My goodness, Jonathan,' she cried. 'You are too bold. I should not be here with you at all at this hour and dressed as I am.' And with that she whisked out of the room and I heard her go upstairs. But though she had reproved me, she had called me by my given name. She had not been severe.

Filled with a surprising joy, I might have sat on in delighted contemplation of a life to be, but I had not done my patrol for some hours now, so was obliged to take up my chilly vigil again. Until morning there was no sign of anything untoward inside or outside the house. I resolved to adopt Cordelia's suggestion. I would lay information against the man on the wharf as early as possible that morning. Some evidence concerning the attack might be got from him and, at all events, once in prison he would not be able to harm anyone.

And it was my dear Cordelia who had clear-headedly gone straight to this solution! I began to dream of a future with her, if only she would consent to marry me. I began to imagine her at Kittering, mistress of my house, tender friend to my sisters, comfort to my father as he grew older. Would she have me? A worldly woman would not have hesitated – but Cordelia was not a worldly woman. She would do only what her heart directed.

I went wearily to bed at six, when the loyal Gilmore took over from me. I thought of Cordelia – my head touched the pillow – I was asleep.

Yet it was not of Cordelia I dreamed. I dreamed instead of that awful figure I had so recently encountered. In my dream he was bare-chested and barefoot on some tropical island under a strong sun. He stood on yellow sand, gazing out over a blue sea. There was the distorted figure, misshapen face, burning eyes and tangled mass of wild black hair. I felt the heart within his breast drumming, sensed the violent movements of his brain, with its capacity for sudden, violent emotion, for good or ill. And then he altered. His face softened and became more regular, his great black eyes ceased to burn like coals and took on a gentler light – he smiled. From somewhere in the trees surrounding the bay I heard a voice, singing. It was the true voice of Maria Clementi, heard in dream, though she was not to be seen. She sang some old mediaeval tune, sombrely yet with great feeling and conviction. It was a song such as one hears in holy processions in Spain and Italy. And the man stood, as if he could not hear her, looking out to sea.

The notes of Maria's song were in my ears as Gilmore, according to my instructions, awoke me at half past seven. Not much later I was on my feet in the dining-room, having taken a cup of coffee from the hand of Cordelia (already up and fresh as a new coin, though silent to her sister on the subject of the night's doings). I intended setting off immediately for the house of Mr Wortley, who lived only a few streets away. At that moment the doorbell jangled and in came my friends Hugo and Lucy, dressed for travelling. This was very strange for the hour was early and there had been nothing about their going the day before. Moreover, few with any choice would set off for Kent with snow on the ground and the chance of more to come.

Invited to take some breakfast Hugo agreed with some relief and urged his wife to sit down and take something. She, however, pale, with two angry red spots on her cheeks, remained standing and shook her head determinedly. Cordelia stood up and, putting an arm round her shoulders, led her to a chair by the fire. She spoke to her softly and evidently induced her to take some cordial.

Mrs Frazer, at the table, gazed at this scene in surprise.

'Well, Hugo,' I asked, 'what brings you here so early?'

Eating heartily, he said, 'I apologise for this early arrival, Mrs Downey, and thank you for your kindness. I regret there is an unhappy affair to discuss.'

'You had better say what it is, Hugo,' I told him.

He glanced at Mrs Frazer, sitting at the table alertly, eyebrows raised, and at Cordelia, standing near his wife.

'I have been made aware of something amiss at Cheyne Walk,' Cordelia then said. Mrs Frazer's eyebrows went further up at this.

It was Lucy who turned her head from the fire and said to her. 'We have left that house.'

'In haste, I assume,' said I.

She stood up again and took a position by the fire, her eyes bright and her whole body rigid with anger. Showing none of Hugo's compunction about what ought or ought not to be discussed before ladies, she exclaimed passionately. 'That woman – that actress – Clementi – arrived at midnight last night. You were right, Jonathan, to accuse Victor of continuing to court that woman when he should have been mourning his poor wife. But what none of us could have known, believed – ah – it's disgraceful – Elizabeth hardly in her grave – monstrous – I told Hugo I could not stay.' And again Cordelia urged her to sit down and calm herself.

With Lucy seated once more Hugo continued the story. 'Let me explain why we could stay no longer at Cheyne Walk. She – the woman Clementi – arrived as Lucy says late last night in a carriage, still in her gold stage dress, her face brightly painted, the very model of a – well, I will spare us all the word. Lucy and I had just gone to our room, but came down again when the bell rang, for it was very late and I had been alarmed Jonathan, by what you said the previous day. She burst in, dressed as I have described, and straight away fell to sobbing in the hall. Victor, who had come from his study, went into something like a frenzy, clasped her to him, told her (for she could say nothing, of course) that some coarse man must have pressed his attentions on her and frightened her, threatened murder, called fire and brimstone on the head of her supposed abuser –

all the while she clung to him, giving no assent or denial to his suppositions about what had brought her to the house. There in the hall in front of Lucy and myself he embraced her, she entwined about him, he told her he loved her, swore he would marry her. And all the while she clung to him, with her painted face turned up to his, allowing him to woo her. Even as we watched, unable to think what to do, he drew her tenderly into the study and closed the door. We heard him turn the key in the lock.'

'He slammed the door, rather, in our faces, without a word,' Lucy exclaimed. 'We would have left then, but it was late, dark and cold. We were forced to sleep there, as much as we could, rose early, packed and left. There was no sign of Victor or the woman.'

'The study door was open as we left,' Hugo reported. 'There was no one in the room. I felt we could not leave London without coming to you, Jonathan, and telling you of this new state of affairs. I was disturbed by your argument yesterday with Victor – and bewildered. But after what we have just seen I ask myself – what am I, what is anybody, to think of Victor Frankenstein? I am sorry, Mrs Downey, to bring this unpleasantness to your house.'

'You are well out of that horrible place,' said Cordelia. 'Jonathan was on his way to lay information against the deformed man of whom he spoke to you yesterday. What you do not know is that when he left you, he saw the fellow climbing over the wall of Mr Frankenstein's house, then bravely followed him to his lair and questioned him.'

'That's more than I would have done,' said Hugo. 'What did he say?'

'The fellow is feeble-witted and hard to understand,' I said, 'but he knows the name of Frankenstein and, my impression was, resents him bitterly. Like you, I do not know what to think.'

As I spoke, there came another jangle at the door-bell and Mrs Frazer, who had sat in amazement as this conversation continued, jumped up to answer it herself, no doubt expecting more alarms – as was the case, for she was almost pushed back into the room by a determined Mrs Jacoby who came through the door like a tornado. Behind her was Gabriel Mortimer, less cock-of-the-walk now, and looking grim.

'Maria – have you seen her?' Mrs Jacoby demanded of me.

'What?' cried Cordelia standing up. 'Who are you? Why do you come here?'

'This is Mrs Jacoby, Miss Clementi's companion, and Mr Mortimer, her impresario,' I explained. 'Mr Mortimer, Mrs Jacoby, this lady rightly asks why you come here, uninvited, at this hour. Do you suppose I have Miss Clementi hidden somewhere in the house?' At that point I confess I was anxious to dispel any impression Cordelia might have that they had any reason to suppose this might be the case.

Mrs Jacoby replied to my question, saying passionately, 'Of course I don't think she's here. But I believe she may be at Frankenstein's. You are his friend.'

'What has that to do with it, Mrs Jacoby?' Cordelia asked.

'The lady is most certainly at Frankenstein's – or was, last night,' Hugo intervened.

'Ah,' Mrs Jacoby said angrily. 'It is just as I thought – just as I told you, Gabriel.' She turned to me, 'Will you go to him and persuade him to release her?' she asked.

Hugo, however, said, 'She went there of her own free will. I and my wife were reluctant witnesses to the scene. She arrived late last night still in her stage dress in a state of great agitation and appeared to be asking for shelter. Which,' he said grimly, 'was granted.'

'That villain!' exclaimed Mortimer. 'What does he want with her?'

'But what do you want with her?' came the clear voice of Cordelia Downey. 'What do either of you want with her?'

There was a silence, broken by Mrs Jacoby, 'You appear to me to be a sensible and respectable woman, and I feel ashamed that the upset of Maria's going has caused Mr Mortimer and I to intrude on you so early.'

'Thank you for your tribute to my character,' Mrs Downey said. 'It does not explain your presence.'

'I must tell you – none of you knows Maria Clementi as I do,' Mrs Jacoby cried out passionately. 'She is the most wicked, immoral creature who ever trod the earth. Come, Gabriel – this is not the place for us. Maria has gone to Frankenstein – did I not tell you that witch was not abducted? Mr Goodall cannot help us. We must go to Cheyne Walk and have it out.' And apologising hastily for their intrusion, the couple left as abruptly as they had arrived, leaving Hugo and Lucy, Cordelia and Mrs Frazer looking at each other in bewilderment.

'There is nothing we can do,' Hugo announced stoutly. 'The woman went to Frankenstein, Frankenstein received her, what more is there to say? We must go, Lucy, now. Mrs Downey, I fear you have had a bad start to your day. I thank you for your hospitality.'

'Well, my dear,' Cordelia said to Lucy Feltham. 'Mr Feltham may be prepared to whisk you breakfastless from the house before you have had a chance to arrange yourself, but I will defy him on your behalf. You must have an egg, hot water, a little cologne and some small chance to restore your equanimity. While all that is taking place my servant can put up some food for your journey and these gentlemen can step round together to the magistrate's to put in hand the matter of the arrest of the imbecile.' She could not resist adding, to me, 'As for the character of Miss Clementi – you now have it from the lips of her own, paid companion.'

We were swept from the house as by a broom leaving the ladies to deal with their arrangements. Mrs Frazer, naturally enough, was bursting with curiosity as to what all the events of the morning might mean. As we walked to Mr Wortley's house Hugo said, 'A woman of some character, your Mrs Downey. You could go further and fare worse –' but I did not reply.

At Mr Wortley's I reported I had reason to suspect that a man who lived on a wharf at Chelsea might have information bearing on the death of Mrs Frankenstein and her child, might indeed be the perpetrator of the crime. Hugo supported this statement and Wortley dispatched men to lay hands on him. I heard from him later that the fellow had decamped during the night. When his workmates arrived in the morning they found him and his very few possessions gone from the hut.

How happy I was during the next weeks. How little I desired gloom, mystery, dreads and doubts. And, though few would have believed it, I was able to banish such thoughts for some weeks as all my tenderness for Cordelia Downey increased and, so she said, did hers for me. Such times are rare and precious for all of us.

Since I was now an admitted lover, it appeared unsuitable for Cordelia, scion of a freedom-loving family though she might have been, to stay alone in the house with her prospective husband. Either I must remove myself or Mrs Frazer stay on as chaperone, and Mrs Frazer having no pressing reason to return home, it was decided she should remain. So, in the light of love offered and returned, small wonder it was possible for me to put darkness from my mind. We planned a visit to my family in Nottingham. I began to forget the frightening and complicated affairs of Victor Frankenstein (who, during this period, did not approach me in friendship, nor I him). When I thought of the affair, I hoped it was over. Alas, this was not to be. Dreadful news arrived all too soon.

ELEVEN

One morning in February the magistrate Mr Wortley arrived, calling me from work on my dictionary to impart some most dreadful news.

Victor Frankenstein lay gravely ill, near death. He had been found, the day before, in the early morning, stabbed as if by a lunatic, in his own drawing-room — that same long, gloomy salon overlooking the garden from which I had observed the lurker, now missing. The window of this room had been broken, exactly as on the night Elizabeth Frankenstein was killed. On the otherwise unbroken snow of the lawn huge, erratic footprints, as if made by a limping man of great stature had been discovered.

Wortley added the dreadful fact that a gardeners' hut near the house bore traces of occupation. Inside was discovered a pile of bedding, some of which had been taken from Victor's house. There was a ragged, black coat, crusts of food lay about, even a plate from the house. Plainly someone had been living in the hut and stealing supplies from Victor's household. Mr Wortley did not doubt that this man was he who had broken in and almost killed Victor, nor that the madman was the very monster I had reported to him.

'While men had been searching everywhere for the culprit,' Wortley said bitterly, 'he was in the last place anyone might have expected to find him – hiding close to his prey. Far from escaping, he had come closer to the man he wished to kill.'

I expressed the utmost horror at this story. I would, I said, go to Victor immediately.

'There is another thing,' Wortley said, a little uncomfortably. 'When the servants raised the alarm they found your friend, bleeding, and a lady with him, a lady who is dumb, cradling him in her arms. I think you will discover she is still there.'

It made a dreadful picture – Victor mortally wounded in that bleak drawing-room at Cheyne Walk, under a broken window, the footprints of his murderer leading away across the white expanse of lawn while Maria, unable to speak or cry out for help, stayed with him as he lay there, near death.

Wortley continued, 'It is unfortunate she cannot speak, for when we catch Mr Frankenstein's attacker – who may, alas, by then be his murderer, for he is between life and death even now – we will need a witness to what happened. But she cannot tell us what she saw. Do you know her? Is there any way she can be got to speak?'

I told him that, to the best of my knowledge, there was not.

I then went to see Victor, accompanied by Cordelia, who offered to give any help she might.

It was very cold but bright as we clopped over hard-packed frozen snow to Cheyne Walk. The sun glinted from the ice of the Thames which was solidly frozen. A ship, sails furled, was trapped in mid-channel; little boys were sliding and whooping on the ice. On the pier where Victor's assassin had once lived and worked, the men had lit a big fire of driftwood round which they stood to warm themselves, though there would be little work for them until the river unfroze.

Victor's butler, a man with an expression of deep doubt and anxiety on his face, opened the door to us, and said he would conduct us to Victor's room. The house was cold, for which he apologised, saying that morning all the maids and the other manservant had left, out of fear. We began to mount the huge, cold staircase to Victor's bedroom, but as we ascended I looked down and through the open door to that large and desolate drawing-room where I observed two burly men sitting on chairs, playing cards. They had been hired, no doubt, to protect the house and Victor from further attack. However, when I commented on this the butler shook his head. 'Would that they had been here last night. I have locked the stable door after the horse has bolted. Alas, the doctor's opinion is that Mr Frankenstein may not have long to live.'

As we reached the landing at the top of the stairs, I was surprised to see seated outside Victor's sick-room the heavily mantled figure of Mrs Jacoby. She stood up as Cordelia and I approached. Her face was very lined; she looked ten years older. She spoke to me with some urgency: 'Mr Goodall, Maria is within, sitting with Mr Frankenstein. But I must speak to you privately – alone.'

'Yes – perhaps,' I said, 'but first let me see poor Victor.' My hand was on the handle of the door.

She grasped me by the arm. 'Make her leave that room,' she urged. 'Mr Goodall – make her leave.'

I entered the vast room where a great fire burned. Victor lay in a four-poster bed, his face turned away from me, looking at Maria, who sat beside him. All the hair was gone from the back of his skull, cut away so as not to clog his wounds. There were two great slashes which had been stitched in black in the form of a cross at the back of his head. His arms lay outside the bedclothes, both heavily bandaged. Mr Wortley had said the weapon used had been a heavy knife, such as cooks employ for large joints of meat. Thirty separate wounds had been made, Wortley said, but of these the most serious would probably be those less visible which had penetrated his chest and stomach.

Maria sat on a chair by the window, clad in a pretty grey dress with a lace fichu at her shoulders. Her hair was arranged in curls on top of her head. She smiled as I approached the bed. She was holding Victor's hand.

I said, 'Victor – Victor – I am desolated to find you like this. What can I do for you?' But Maria, with a little wave of her small hand, attracted my attention and, wearing a small, rueful smile, pointed at Victor, then at her own mouth, shaking her head. I did not take her meaning at first, so she went through the pantomime again. This time I understood. 'He cannot speak?' I questioned. She shook her head again.

I went round the bed to the side where she sat, to show him my concern, even if it was impossible to speak to him. I gazed down at that grey, wasted face and was appalled by what I saw.

Maria had his hand in hers, his eyes were upon her face – and on his face was an expression of absolute horror. He gazed into that pretty face as if he were looking into the pits of hell. She continued to smile gently at him, then bent gracefully to kiss him on the brow. A puff of smoke caused by some back draught came from the fireplace into the room. For a moment I saw, as if in a dream, smoke curling round Maria, and the prone figure of Frankenstein.

I thought of Mrs Jacoby's appeal to me to make Maria leave the sick-room. I dropped to my knees beside the bed (which inevitably meant that Maria had to let go of Victor's hand) and put my face to his, saying, 'My dear fellow – my very dear fellow – are you afraid, what is the matter?'

His eyes met mine in fear and underneath I thought I saw an appeal. I glanced at Maria, who shook her head, smiled and indicated by her expression that what I saw was not to be taken seriously. I gazed deep into her inexpressive, lovely eyes and felt I was drowning. I wrenched my own eyes away and they fell on Victor's fearful face.

'Victor,' I appealed. 'Can you tell me what ails you?' But he could not, though he seemed to be pleading with me. Then, as if he had been mesmerised, his gaze, frightened, yet in some way obedient like a beaten child's, went back to Maria.

'Miss Clementi,' I said. 'I know you mean well, but

it appears to me that your presence in this sick-room is disturbing Victor in some way. Would it not be better to end your visit and return at a later time?' She smiled directly into my eyes – a pang, most shameful in these circumstances, went through me. I thought, I am mad. I must be mad. Then she bent her pitying look on the invalid, whose hand she took again in her own, and at that his face seemed to become more ashen, more lined, if that were possible. I was forced to say again, 'I truly think your presence agitates him. A man as ill as Victor must be indulged, or his recovery will be slowed.' Or never take place at all was what I meant, though I did not say so. 'Why do you not leave him now,' I continued, 'and return tomorrow, when perhaps he will be a little stronger.'

But she only smiled and shook her head and held the hand of the terrified man. She would not leave.

I flung myself from the room, finding Mrs Jacoby in sympathetic conversation with Cordelia, as if the unpleasant early morning interview at Gray's Inn Road had never taken place. I exclaimed, 'Mrs Jacoby, she makes love to him even as he lies there dying, but his eyes are full of fear when he looks at her! She terrifies him. He pleads wordlessly with me to make her go but she will not – will not. He has conceived some irrational fear of her. She must leave him.'

'That was why I asked you to try to get her from the room,' Mrs Jacoby said. 'She has been with him now for a day and a half, ever since he was attacked.'

'Can you not influence the doctor to force her out and install some determined nurse to stay with

Mr Frankenstein all the time?' Cordelia asked. 'One must pander to the fancies of a man so ill.'

'Fancies? – These are no fancies,' replied Mrs Jacoby, grimly. 'I told the doctor yesterday of this, but he was taken in, no doubt by Maria's pretty face. Mr Goodall – he comes in an hour. Will you speak to him?'

'I will,' I said. 'But should not Victor's parents be here to direct matters now he is so ill?'

'Mrs Jacoby tells me he will not have them called,' Cordelia told me.

'Is it right to be guided by him over that? I doubt it. He is very ill and his judgment may be affected. I am sure they would wish to be here.'

Mrs Jacoby said, 'All I know is that Maria must be excluded from the sick-room.'

I felt I could hardly bear to re-enter the room and look again into the terrified eyes staring desperately from that grey and wasted face. Yet I forced myself to do so, crossing the room to where Maria sat, still clutching Victor's hand. I assured him I would speak to the doctor as soon as he came and that we would get a capable nurse to be with him all the time. Having said that, which I thought from his expression relieved his mind somewhat, I cast a glance at Maria, who smiled as ever. Was there malice in her eyes or did I imagine it?

After I left the room Cordelia took my arm and said, 'Mrs Jacoby must speak to you.' I followed her downstairs to that long, cold salon with its shrouded chandeliers and fading light. A couple of candles stood on the mantelpiece where a pathetic fire burned. As we came in the two guards leapt up as if to appear vigilant. We stood away from them by the window, conversing in low tones, possibly on the very spot where Victor had lain, stabbed, after the attack.

Outside the snow still lay on the branches of the trees and on the grass. Now the ground was covered with the marks of frozen footprints, left by the belated search for Frankenstein's attacker. But the searchers had gone – I only wondered, had the man for whom they searched returned? Was he out there, his body pressed against the black trunk of a tree?

Then Mrs Jacoby grasped my arm – I felt her fingers pressing hard into my flesh, in spite of my coat. She said urgently, 'I can stay silent no longer. You must know the truth, I must tell you everything about Maria Clementi.'

TWELVE

Mrs Jacoby's face was very strained as she said, 'You must hear what I have to say now, for tomorrow I leave Miss Clementi's service. Would that I had gone sooner. I have stayed on with her, though, God knows, my conscience has urged me over and over again to leave. Why did I stay? For the money, I confess. She paid me well. And because, in my vanity, I thought I did more good than harm by staying and even – vain hope – believed I could convert her, eventually into a reasonable human being, a creature with a heart and with a soul. But now I must tell you everything about her.'

'You are very bitter, Mrs Jacoby,' Cordelia said. 'Pray, do not say too much in the heat of your anger and disappointment with Miss Clementi – '

'There is no heat to my anger,' Mrs Jacoby interrupted. 'Nor to my distress, nor my loathing of that abominable creature. I am stone cold. I have been with her for years. I have seen all her doings. I have no feeling left but disgust. Maria Clementi,' she went on, 'is immoral, profoundly immoral by any normal standards, yet I believe she is actually beyond morality, if any mortal can be. She is evil – yet I believe she does not know, she does not understand what she does. She is a savage – perhaps even worse than a savage, for we read that savages have their society, their laws, their taboos, however strange. Maria is secretly cruel: she steals, if she thinks she will not be caught; she is a libertine, but conceals it. She cares not what she does, only whether she will be found out. And I – I have helped to hide what she does.'

'Mortimer is her lover?' Mrs Downey asked calmly, as if asking the price of fish. I thought, he cannot be – that venal, shady creature cannot be Maria's lover – but Mrs Jacoby answered, 'Yes. Of course he is. He and a hundred others. I have been with her for five years in all the capitals of Europe and there have always been men, too many to count. Some loved her, poor creatures, their sufferings were the worst. She did not know how she wounded them. How could she, for she cannot give or receive love? I have seen dogs with more apparent love and loyalty. As to the rest, I cannot tell you all the terrible things she has done and which I, for my sins, have helped her conceal.

'There was a beggar woman in Vienna, a poor woman with a child in her arms who stopped Maria nightly as she entered the opera house asking for money. This woman Maria could not abide. She began by kicking the woman when she begged of her. But the woman persisted. One evening, as she was entering the theatre, Maria fell on that woman – and her child – in a frenzy.

She tore at the woman's eyes and there was blood all over her face – and Maria's hands. The child fell to the ground – doctors had to be called. Silence cost us dear. It was in Vienna too, on another occasion, when she thought the director of the theatre was favouring another singer over her – this woman was given a song Maria thought was hers, she was put in the centre of the stage where Maria thought she should be. Perhaps the director was her lover and favouring his mistress. Maria put lime in the cream the other actress used to clean her face. Imagine the pain and deformity with which that woman was left. Even in Dublin, where she was first found, they told me she had killed a man among the people with whom she then lived. Perhaps she had some cause. Perhaps he had attacked her but – oh – I have seen her close to murder so many times that I would not be sure she had any good cause to kill the man.

'You see,' Mrs Jacoby said, 'Maria is unlike anyone in the world. She is violent, vengeful, without remorse. I have tried to control her. I have covered up her misdeeds. But this affair with Mr Frankenstein is the end. I knew she wanted him – but why? Yet, as she wanted him, she had him. She is skilled at the measures of the old dance – as he moved forward, she moved back, but only so far as to be nearly within reach. Then he moved forward again and she, with the appearance of the utmost purity and virtue, moved away again – but only to bring him further on. She knew she must do that, for if she yielded too soon he would value her less. And thus she hooked him and even now as he lies on what may be his deathbed she sucks the life out of him.

'I have borne enough; she has bought five years of my life at a price I should never have agreed – the price, almost, of my soul.' She paused for a moment, the cold winter light on her drained face. She was no longer the capable woman I had first met. 'Why?' she questioned. 'Why, having enticed him, does she wish to torment him? I have thought sometimes her evil ways were the result of her upbringing, mute and defenceless among Irish tinkers, though not of them. She was untaught, used to beg and sing for money in the streets. I had thought to help and improve her, make her more gentle in spirit, but now, after five years, she is more ruthless and immoral than before. This refusal to leave Mr Frankenstein's sick-bed is vile, a new vileness, I cannot understand it. I will not bear it. I must leave.'

'But where will you go?' I asked.

'To my sister's in Chatham, today,' she told me. 'She is a widow on a small pension. There will be little money and she is an adherent of a narrow, canting sect. I expect to have their pastor with me continually exhorting me to wash in the blood of the Lamb. It will not be a pleasant life, but better, better by far, than that with Maria Clementi. I leave you to protect Mr Frankenstein from her attentions.'

Cordelia then asked, 'Who is she? Where did she first come from? You must have some knowledge of what made her what she is? What of these gypsies, or tinkers?'

'It was Gabriel Mortimer who found her at the house of friends in Dublin, where they had her to sing after supper. She had been singing and begging in the street for some time before that, and due to the sweetness of her voice and her beauty it came to be the habit of some of the better families to hire her to perform for them in the evenings after supper. The beautiful gypsy, they called her. At that time she was in the charge of a dirty old woman who controlled her comings and goings and I'm sure took her wages from her when she was paid. That woman may have been a tinkerwoman or have bought her from tinkers. Anyhow neglect and cruelty must have been Maria's portion. Sometimes she screams aloud at night, as I confided to you, Mr Goodall. Sometimes she will sit and stare with clouded eyes as if recollecting some scene from the past. But because she cannot speak she is locked away from ordinary discourse with others, as a prisoner is locked away, and for that reason I believe she lives much in the past, even as a prisoner will. For that I pity her. But for nothing else.

'I came into her employment as a result of Mr Mortimer's visit to some members of my husband's family in Merrion Square. I was staying with them and had become used to the occasional visits of Maria, who was brought to the house by the old woman of whom I have spoken. Even then she had a fastidious nature, for considering her condition she was as clean as a cat, and of course able to sing most beautifully, not just in English and French but also the old Erse songs. One could not understand the words of them, yet listening one found oneself almost weeping. She had, you see, a facility, perhaps compensating her for her dumbness – she could learn any piece of music after hearing it only once.

'Then we come to Gabriel Mortimer. He was visiting my brother-in-law having some business with him

touching a joint share in a trading venture in Canada
– this on the verge of going wrong (Mortimer has a
finger in many pies; money is his god). He heard the
girl sing and there was I, on a soldier's widow's pension,
vigorous and lacking occupation – who better to act as
the girl's guide and companion when Mortimer rapidly
decided to take her to London for her debut? I believe
he bought her from the old woman.

'At first all went well. She was pleased to be well
housed and fed and not beaten – her body was and is
badly marked by beatings. On her arm there is a scar
where she was pushed or fell into a fire as a child. She
most rapidly learned the manners of those in a better
way of life, how to comport herself and to dress and
to behave abroad and at table. Her progress was so
rapid I wondered if she might have been at one time
locked away by a respectable family ashamed of her
deficiency in speech, given away or stolen away from
her parents, unable to cry out. That might account for
her aptitude in learning so quickly the niceties of life.
But it was not long before her evil ways emerged – she
would steal anything and everything, always with the
utmost skill. She was cruel, wantonly needlessly cruel,
as if possessed. To try to make her love something, even
if she could love no human being, I tried the experiment
of getting her a little dog. She burned its body, artfully
hiding the burns for as long as she could. When I found
out, the wounds had festered – Mortimer and I had to
have it killed.

And her behaviour was lewd, debauched. Not two
months after we reached London Mortimer was her
lover – I daresay he was after two days but I did

not suspect until later. Though when I say he was her lover I do not mean there was love involved in the affair. On his side, low as he is, there may have been some – on hers, none. She took him as an animal will, with no thought but to satisfy her base desires. She is not, however, exclusive. Those looking for her relationships with Lord This or the Count of That will find nothing. Thus, as well as due to my help, she retains her reputation for extraordinary purity in a profession not given over to virtue. No – if you wish to find out where Maria Clementi disposes of her body, go to the waterfronts of any of the capital cities of Europe, go to the stews, go into the filthiest parts of the towns – there you will find her, with one man, or many. I will spare you more. I have said enough already before Mrs Downey. Leave it that she is the foulest creature who ever walked the earth.

'Mercifully, we were always moving from city to city – from Vienna to Rome, from Rome to Budapest. Had that not been the case much trouble would have come to us. Mortimer and I, in conspiracy, by bribery and by continually moving on, were able to hide what she did. All the while we pretended Maria was an angel – and all the while I knew I was protecting, was paid to protect, a woman who, thwarted, prevented or annoyed in any way, reacted by attacking the source of her pain without any consideration at all, who saw no reason not to take what she wanted, hurt whom she wished to hurt, without any remorse. I do not know how long it is,' Mrs Jacoby said, 'since I realised I had lost all hope of influencing her for good. I know that for too long I have eaten her bread and quenched my conscience.'

As this confession continued I wished my dear Cordelia absent. Mrs Jacoby's tale, as she had said, was unsuitable for her ears. However, inasmuch as I could tell what Cordelia, who listened intently, was thinking, she showed no signs of shock or horror. She now said, 'My dear Mrs Jacoby, if what you say is true, you have been in a most unusual situation, one you could not have prepared for, and must have had much difficulty in understanding.'

'Well,' said Mrs Jacoby, fastening her bonnet strings and folding her mantle firmly about her, 'thank you for those words. I must now go to earn my forgiveness in Chatham and regret I shall have to leave the business of the doctor to you, for, to be honest, I hope never to hear the names of Mr Frankenstein and, above all, that of Maria Clementi, ever again. I go to do my penance now, but, before I go, I warn you, if you become any further involved in this matter you may find yourselves having to do your own penance later. This affair is damnable and may entangle the best of individuals like weed dragging them down to the bottom.' And with that she turned abruptly, crossed the long room and went out, leaving us standing in that cold room together.

Cordelia gazed after the departing figure, then turned to me and asked, 'Jonathan? Do you believe what Mrs Jacoby says?'

'I do not fully know,' I answered her, 'but it is as well we are due in Nottingham as soon as the weather is sufficiently improved for us to make the journey. We cannot disappoint my family, who dearly wish to meet you and I long to take you to my home. And in that way I do what I ought, and dearly desire to do and we take Mrs Jacoby's parting advice also. We will be far away from London soon.'

Cordelia said, 'Will you not call for Mr Frankenstein's parents? They ought to be with him – and may manage to keep that viper from his side. But I will see Mrs Jacoby before she leaves.' I did not ask her what she hoped to discover by a further conversation with the lady.

When the doctor arrived I urged him in the strongest terms to ensure Victor had nurses day and night and that Maria Clementi was not allowed near the sick man at any time.

We had taken a carriage home and it was there that Cordelia, one small cold hand in mine, said, with some diminution of her normal confidence, 'I am afraid of all this, Jonathan, and not for fear of any madman coming to murder us. I dread further entanglement in Mr Frankenstein's affairs may end our joy, destroy our love.'

I laughed and called her a goose.

THIRTEEN

That evening, we sat at our fireside. The ladies sewed and rather than dwell upon the melancholy and alarming events of that gloomy house in Chelsea, we spoke rather of our forthcoming visit to Kittering Hall. Mrs Frazer then recalled she had been invited to attend a private performance by Mr Augustus Wheeler one evening the following week at the house of a friend, a titled Scottish lady residing in London. On account of our journey, she said, she would be obliged to tell her friend she could not come. Cordelia said she considered this a great sacrifice.

A scientist as well as a showman, Augustus Wheeler had been causing much interest with his displays on the London stage and in private homes over the past few months. Audiences had been delighted and horrified by his power over those members of his audience – apparently unknown to him – who, having been subjected to his mesmeric powers, crowed like cocks, walked about the stage on their hands, delivered long poems they claimed earlier to have forgotten and all manner of such things. Some called Wheeler a charlatan, while others were entirely convinced by him. Others still pointed to the cosultations he conducted in private, for a fee, at which he cured people of stammering, bashfulness and, in the case of one lady, of an apparent inability ever to leave her own front door without fainting. The newspapers debated the truth of mesmerism; clerics warned their congregations against his displays; Wheeler was a celebrity. He was invited to great men's houses and entertained many important persons with his displays.

Said I to Mrs Frazer, 'You would not, I hope, have offered yourself for a demonstration.'

'Good heavens, no,' she exclaimed, 'I have no wish to be seen clucking like a chicken in front of half London.'

'Do you think the man a fraud?' Cordelia asked Mrs Frazer.

'I do not know what to think,' she responded.

'What of you, Jonathan?' Cordelia asked me.

'There is much evidence to say it is true,' I answered. 'Yet it violates our belief in man's free will if one man can mesmerise another and persuade him to do things he would ordinarily eschew.'

'That is what is so frightening,' mused Cordelia. There was a silence and then it was as though we two thought as one, for, just as Cordelia began, in a thoughtful tone, 'Miss Clementi – ' I myself said, 'I wonder if Mr Wheeler – ' and we stared at each other in, as the poet says, 'wild surmise' and both fell silent again.

'Come, come, the pair of you,' Mrs Frazer said.

'You know you must not start sentences without finishing them.'

I said, 'I believe Cordelia and I both thought at the same moment that Mr Wheeler might be the last hope of restoring Maria Clementi's powers of speech. She has seen many doctors and other eminent men of science, but so far none has been able to help her. Surely it is at least possible that a man who can make a lifelong stammerer cease to stutter, as Wheeler has, and has performed many other apparent miracles, might have some effect on Miss Clementi. Is that not so – is that not what you were about to suggest, Cordelia?'

Cordelia nodded and Mrs Frazer said, 'Maybe so. But why do you want to do anything for that nasty creature?'

'She is the only person who may know what happened on the night Victor Frankenstein was attacked. She may have seen his assailant. But she cannot speak and Mr Wortley says even if they lay hands on the villain and accuse him of murder, there is a chance the jury will pronounce him innocent, as there is insufficient evidence.'

'Surely that cannot be true,' Mrs Frazer said. 'Here is a man, half a beast, who has been haunting Mr Frankenstein's house. Mrs Frankenstein has been murdered, Frankenstein himself attacked – how could they declare the man not guilty?'

'Wortley knows his juries,' said I. 'He tells me they can behave most unpredictably, especially when, as in this case, there are no other witnesses to the man's guilt.'

'If they ever find him,' Mrs Frazer said tartly.

'If they do,' said I.

'Nevertheless,' Cordelia said, 'if Mr Wheeler could assist Miss Clementi to speak, what might she not be able to tell of the attacker?'

'I imagined I heard you say earlier we should have no more to do with the affair,' I said, pretending confusion.

'And that I most sincerely believe,' Cordelia responded. 'Yet a lady may think two things at the same time and go unchallenged. Poor Mr Frankenstein needs any help we can give up before we leave for Nottingham.'

'Then I will speak to Mr Wortley tomorrow,' I said. 'He may consider any attempt to get evidence against the assassin worthwhile. But then comes the matter of persuading Miss Clementi to accept the treatment. I suppose there will be no trouble with Wheeler. He will welcome the notoriety such an attempt would bring. But to persuade Maria Clementi without the stabilising influence of Mrs Jacoby – ' And there was another sentence left unfinished.

I saw Wortley next day and, though initially startled by the proposition that testimony might be got from Maria by the intervention of a mesmerist, he agreed that information from any source was better than none at all. He added that it was after all my affair and Miss Clementi's if we chose to seek the help of Mr Wheeler.

That afternoon Cordelia and I set off for Cheyne Walk and, on our arrival, were somewhat astonished to hear that Miss Clementi was again upstairs with Mr Frankenstein. Had not the doctor given explicit instructions that Miss Clementi be not allowed in the sick-room, I demanded of the manservant? He looked at me helplessly, but did not reply.

'She has got round the nurse,' Cordelia declared in an undertone as we set off up the stairs. 'I believe she must be one of the cleverest women in England.'

Her prediction was all too true. When we reached Victor's chamber door the nurse was seated outside. Recalling the dreadful fear on Victor's face I had seen last time Maria was with him, I lost my temper with the woman and asked her harshly had she not heard the doctor say Miss Clementi was not to be allowed into the sick-room? What now possessed her to run against the doctor's orders? The nurse, evidently seduced by Maria's fame and charm of person, responded with some rambling tale about never having seen before such sweet and selfless devotion, she had heard the sick man calling for her and much rubbish of that kind.

'Go in and ask her to come out,' I ordered.

But she would not. Happily at that moment the doctor arrived, visited Victor in his room and came out with a compliant and sweetly smiling Maria. The nurse was discharged and Cordelia went to get a good woman of whom she knew.

'This is a most difficult situation,' the doctor told me. 'There is no one here to take charge. Mr Frankenstein's condition is very grave.'

'I have sent for Mr Frankenstein's parents,' I told him and then turned to Maria, still standing by, and asked if I might have a private word with her.

She had evidently organised the household to her liking, for she led me to the little parlour which had once been Mrs Frankenstein's and there I found a good fire burning and, over the fireplace, a portrait of Maria herself, satined and bejewelled, as Aeneas' jilted lover, Dido, painted by Sir Thomas Lawrence. This shocked me, though I said nothing. Instead, I explained to her, as clearly as I could, that it might be that Mr Augustus Wheeler, by mesmerising her, could restore her lost powers of speech. She appeared to understand completely, knew the name of Wheeler and charmingly mimicked his work by closing her eyes and laying her pretty head sideways on her hands. I added it was felt she might be able to help with the investigation into Victor's assailant, should she be able to speak. Again she smiled nodded and showed every willingness to help. Would she, I asked, permit me to talk to Mr Wheeler about the matter and see if he agreed with our plan? To this she agreed, indicating to me by gestures she would not be found at Cheyne Walk but (pointing) at Russell Square henceforth. Plainly, she had decided to abandon Cheyne Walk and return to her own home (picture as well, I suppose).

'Very well,' said I to her, 'I will find you there when I have spoken to Wheeler,' and I began to take leave of her. She was all happiness, with the gaiety of a child and charm a woman in one. She came up to me, put her little hands on my shoulders and lifted her face for a kiss. I kissed her brow, then stepped back quickly, for the urge to take her in my arms was almost irresistible. I found myself beginning to mistrust the account of her given by Mrs Jacoby, though I knew I would not confide my doubts to Cordelia.

I returned to Gray's Inn Road where my bride-to-be awaited me. There we sat down to talk, hand in hand. Cordelia smiled at me a little wearily. 'How I yearn for all this to be over and done with and you and I married and living peacefully together, I keeping your house, you taking care of your land and completing the work on your dictionary.'

I felt a terrible tiredness wash over me like a wave and could scarcely answer her.

Meanwhile, whether Mrs Frazer had engagements or no, we were unable to leave London. It froze hard, snowed, then froze for over a week. There was no question of making the journey of one hundred miles to Nottingham in such conditions. A man on horseback would have had a very hard time of it and to journey in a carriage containing two ladies and a child would have been madness. Beggars froze to death in their doorways, birds froze on their branches. It was a hard year when we felt spring would never come.

I used the time to write to Augustus Wheeler at his theatre, telling him what I was sure he must know, of the mysterious muteness of Maria Clementi and asking if he would contemplate making a last attempt to restore her powers of speech. I added he might be aware she had been present at the time of the maniacal attack on Mr Victor Frankenstein, and therefore might have some information to give as to the identity of the criminal. The undertaking, I said forcibly, must be entirely private and not used to enlarge his name.

The very next day an answer came from Mr Wheeler, thanking me for my confidence, stating that he would be very happy to attempt to restore Miss Clementi's voice by mesmerism and assuring me he would observe the utmost confidentiality over the experiment. He made some references to the power of mesmerism and added that if I or Miss Clementi would care to attend what he called 'a demonstration in mesmerism' at the theatre one night he would be pleased to present us with tickets. His writing, I observed, was flowery and ornate; the ink he used the palest blue. I guessed from this flamboyance he must be only part scientist, the rest showman.

That settled, I sent a message to Gabriel Mortimer at Russell Square, telling him I would call on him on a matter of importance the following afternoon, unless I heard from him earlier that he would be away from home.

Next day I went there and I was shown into a sitting-room on the first floor of the house, which overlooked the icy branches, laden with snow, of the trees in the square outside. A bright fire burned in the room, which was charming, decorated with pictures, delicate furniture and bright carpets. I observed the portrait of Maria as Dido on the wall opposite the fireplace. She and her painted representation had evidently re-established themselves at Russell Square. The lady who was seated, sewing, when I entered, put her work away and got up to greet me, both hands outstretched. Mortimer remained in his chair, legs extended to the fire, as Maria put both soft hands in mine.

I could not convict her. I was not even sure I should. Was I to reject her on Mrs Jacoby's words alone? Had there not been, perhaps, a grievance between the two, resulting in Mrs Jacoby's dismissal and her subsequent bitterness? Even the look of fear on Victor's face as Maria sat by him – might that not be caused by pain or terror of death, rather than by the woman sitting near him?

Nonetheless, I reflected that Gabriel Mortimer seemed more at home in this house than perhaps he ought, Maria being without the chaperonage of Mrs Jacoby. Yet this need not mean the pair were lovers; these were after all stage folk, made intimate in special ways by long and arduous journeys together and all the alarms and excitements of their trade. I was not a censorious old woman – Maria Clementi might merely be unwise not depraved. These were my thoughts at the time – I told myself what I wished to beleive.

I briefly gave my message, that Augustus Wheeler would be happy to mesmerise Miss Clementi in the hope of restoring her powers of speech. Gabriel Mortimer, in spite of his foppish appearance – on this day he sported green velveteen trousers and a butter-coloured waistcoat, over which spread a watch-chain thick and heavy enough to rival the Lord Mayor of London's chain of office – took my point. He stood up, went to Maria and, looking down on her, asked her earnestly if it was true she wished to try the experiment with Wheeler. She nodded eagerly. He questioned her again, urgently, did she understand what he could do, put her to sleep, tell her to speak, did she understand she would have no control over herself while she was in his power, that, in the end, sadly, the attempt could fail?

She smiled, stood up, twirled round gracefully, a delighted child looking forward to a treat. She smiled at me radiantly. Poor creature, I thought, how hard her life must have been, from her beginnings as a mute, exploited girl in Ireland to her present existence of continual travel and performance. I compared the lot of my sisters, sheltered and protected from all harm, with Maria's. How hard it must have been, leading such a life, to be unable to speak, to express herself, or to communicate with others. Her existence, though filled with applause and heaps of golden guineas, lacked gentleness and solace. No wonder she now danced, I thought, with her skirts sailing round her, her motions light and feathery, her smile full of innocent pleasure.

Seconds later she was at my chair, gazing down at me, still smiling, her great eyes with those enormously dilated pupils fixed on mine. I felt, I confess, a surge of passion for her which I simultaneously wished to deny. It was an urge to succumb to her to which I knew I must not yield. I greatly feared that small, light creature, frail but strong. And I knew she knew all I was feeling – and rejoiced.

I took a hasty leave of her and Mortimer, wondering if they laughed at me once I was down in the street. I walked home, cursing myself for a fool, resolving never to see her again nor have anything to do with her. It would not take much for her to ruin me, as she had ruined poor Victor. That innocence was false, she had deceived me, Maria Clementi was a serpent. As I walked I began to wonder ruefully if Wheeler would succeed in mesmerising her or would she, with those great eyes, mesmerise him?

Once home I discovered Cordelia and Mrs Frazer were off visiting, attended by the faithful Gilmore – and was pleased for once to find them away from the house, for I was thoroughly shaken and ashamed of myself and needed time to recover from that great wave of sick desire and the equally strong impulse of resistance. Time, and past the time to be gone from London, I thought I had done what I could and now it was for Mortimer and Wheeler to put their heads together and decide how the matter of the mesmerism should go on.

Then mercifully the thaw came and by the end of February sun and wind had cleared the thaw, or most of it, and the roads were open again. Our decision was made – we would take Mrs Frazer's coach North. Cordelia, myself and little Flora would at last get to Nottingham, Mrs Frazer would spend a few days with us and then, with Gilmore as ever, proceed home to Scotland.

Late in the evening before our departure the hall was full of corded boxes, young Flora was up and down from her bed crying out she was unable to sleep, and Cordelia busy giving instructions to her maid and cook, who were to stay behind to mind the house. Just then a servant brought me a message from Mr Wheeler. I opened this missive, addressed in his flourishing blue ink.

'*Sir,*' the letter began.

'*I have had a first encounter with Miss Clementi and am satisfied she can speak! This is most wonderful and surprising to me. But I am afraid to go further with our meetings as I am most alarmed. Will you meet me urgently for I must discuss this matter with you. Mr Mortimer is all for going on with the experiments, but I am doubtful and, alas, cannot think of anyone other than yourself to consult. May I therefore take the liberty of calling tomorrow at noon? Please let me know if this is not convenient to you. At all events I beg for an early interview.*'

Yet we were eagerly expected at Kittering Hall by my father and sisters and my sister's intended husband,

and this was the occasion on which I was to introduce Cordelia as my wife-to-be. Having been already detained by bad weather, I could not allow an occasion so important to all of us to be postponed again.

I knew, too, that I must resist the temptation to have any more to do with Maria. If I did, I could lose all. Worse, I could lose all, and not care what I lost.

Accordingly I left a note with Cordelia's servant telling Wheeler we had left for a journey and he might write to me if he chose at Kittering. Thus we departed Gray's Inn Road next morning early, leaving behind the glooms, the frights – and perhaps, just as importantly, the temptations – of London.

FOURTEEN

We made steady speed, with Gilmore at the reins, though the carriage was heavily laden. Flora, who had done little travelling in her life, was full of excitement and I was pleased to see that the journey put my dear Cordelia in good heart, in spite, perhaps, of her being a little nervous of her reception by her new family.

As we moved North in cold but sparkling weather, my restlessness and anxiety began to abate.

We decided to put up at an inn half-way and it was here, as Gilmore and I occupied ourselves with the horses in the stables, that he turned to me and asked for more news of Frankenstein. He had heard of the attack, of course, as had all London. I told him what I could. He said only, 'I truly believe that the poor creature which the doctor kept locked up on Orkney was a man, however degraded his condition, and that the fellow has come back for him.'

I responded I thought he might be right and we should all thank God we were away from London. To this he assented heartily.

When we arrived at Kittering my father, Arabella and Anna were there to give us a warm welcome. Also at the house was the good Dudley Hight, who would marry Arabella in May. Mrs Frazer stayed on with us for a few days, so we were a large and merry party. Little Flora rejoiced in the freedom of having a large house and a whole estate to roam in, rapidly becoming a favourite of my father's estate manager, who found a pony from somewhere and was soon taking her round with him, he in front on his big bay, she plugging on behind on Tansy, as her pony was called. On one memorable night, not long after our arrival, they went out to watch badgers play under the moon.

I cannot speak too highly of the warmth of the greeting given Cordelia by my father and sisters. I knew – who could not have? – that my father had hopes of a better match for me, in worldly terms, than a solicitor's poor widow, with a growing girl of her own. Yet he welcomed her cordially and full-heartedly, taking an instant liking to her, as did my sisters. It was no disadvantage that my father soon discovered what neither Cordelia nor I had found out ourselves – that he had been at Trinity with her father, John Jessop. We laughed much over dinner to hear of the capers they had had in their university days. We found the college had rechristened Cordelia's father Radical Jack in his youth because of the nature of his views. It would seem that Jack had kept a couple of wolfhounds in his room and a pair of hawks, which had not delighted either his fellow students or the college authorities. There had been all kinds of roistering, gaming and running up of debts in the circles in which father and Jack Jessop had moved, enough to make me rueful, when I recalled the many admonitory letters I had received from my watchful parent during my college days.

So there was laughter, there were visits from neighbours and kinsfolk in the locality and comings and goings from one house to another. Among the ladies, of course, was much exchange of patterns, discussions of the latest style and countless demonstrations of stitchings, launderings, tuckings, ruchings and gopherings – all matters mysterious to men and giving some answer to the mystery of why ladies have, mercifully, so little energy left over from their interests to devote to deep study and philosophical speculation. So there were four days of pleasure and gaiety until some five days after our arrival, when, like a cloud coming over a perfect day, another disturbing letter arrived from Augustus Wheeler.

That morning we were to go hunting, the hunt due to assemble at Kittering Hall. All was excitement and flurry, Flora had been up since daybreak, having been given leave to follow the hunt on her pony from a safe distance. Dressed for riding we broke our fast from laden tables, with whatever neighbours had arrived betimes. Meanwhile outside the house was confusion as grooms brought up our saddled horses or held the mounts of the early-comers. It was a bright morning and we all looked keenly forward to the day. In the midst of all, a boy came up from the village with letters.

Even as servants cleared the tables and others carried

round hot punch to the mounted riders outside, even as
I heard the baying of the hounds being brought up the
drive to the house, I opened Wheeler's letter, suddenly
gloomy, suspecting the happy days at Kittering had been
only a respite from the affairs of Victor Frankenstein,
not an ending of them.

Whatever the message, though, I declared to myself,
I would not leave Kittering. The letter read:

'*My dear Mr Goodall,*

'*I much regret having missed you in London and
now consider it most necessary to communicate to you
the strange and alarming results of my first encounter
with Miss Clementi, whom you asked me to visit. I am
sorry to disturb you in this way but you must, and I
think would wish, to hear of this, since you were good
enough to suggest I might be able to help her.*

'*First I should say that in the past I have been asked
to bring my powers to bear on certain mystifying cases
where there is no seeming cause for the patient's affliction. In attempting to relieve these conditions, much
like any Physician, I have had my cures, my failures and
those apparent successes which do not endure because,
after a brief remission, the sufferer lapses back into
his previous condition. But I have never experienced
anything like what I met with on my visit to Miss
Clementi, not because it was a failure – indeed, the
encounter contained promise of future success. But it
was very alarming, so much so that I am anxious about
continuing my treatment.*

'*I went to Miss Clementi's house in Russell Square
on February 19th, the day before I sought my interview
with you. I arrived at about half past two and was*

welcomed by Miss Clementi herself and her impresario Mr Mortimer. Another gentleman, never introduced to me, arrived a little later and was present with Mr Mortimer during the proceedings.

'I would have preferred another lady, some relative or trusted companion, to be present – indeed I had assumed such a person would be there. Had I foreseen what would occur I would have insisted. But as it was, although I found the absence of any lady and the presence of Mr Mortimer and the young gentleman a little unusual, I saw no reason to object. I recognised the unknown gentleman as having been present at one of my exhibitions at a private house, though I did not then know his name.

'It may have been Miss Clementi herself was not fully at ease in this situation. At any rate she proved singularly hard to mesmerise. My method is, in accordance with established practice, to persuade the object of my study to sink into a trance by the swinging of some object (I use a crystal on a silver chain) before his eyes while speaking to him in a low voice, thus relaxing his mind and persuading him into the necessary state of trance.

'As I swung the crystal on its chain before her, Miss Clementi sat in one chair, while I sat opposite in a similar chair, drawn up close. During this exercise Mr Mortimer and his friend stood against a wall close to the door, to witness this procedure, acting in a most deplorable and quite unsuitable way, talking loudly to each other and at one point calling for wine. This undesirable atmosphere may also have made its contribution to the difficulty I found in having any effect on Miss Clementi. She was not an easy subject

for mesmerism. The normal individual approaching mesmerism will either be willing to comply, or adopt a kind of nervous defiance of it, the former attitude being more common with ladies, the latter, with gentlemen. Miss Clementi reacted in neither of these ways but sat in her chair, charmingly, regarding the swinging crystal with a kind of neutral interest.

'I presumed that, hardened by her own work on the stage, she believed at bottom my scientific experiments in mesmerism to be some form of illusion, as with a magician or conjuror. In vain I swung the crystal to and fro before her, uttering what some have called my "incantations" (in fact a mélange of suggestions to her that she should repose herself and fall into a reverie).

'At one point, the crystal proving ineffective, I asked her to look into my own eyes, hoping thus to influence her. This I ceased to do, for, when she turned her gaze to mine I saw an emptiness in her eyes which alarmed me. They were like great dark pools, the pupils being much enlarged. They were almost, at that moment, if I dare say it, like the eyes of an animal, quite inhuman. I suspected for a moment, I confess, that she was turning the tables on me – attempting to entrance me.'

Here, I think, I laid the letter down on the mantelpiece. The room had emptied. Through the long windows I could see, on the grass outside, the crowd of horsemen and those who would follow on foot. The hounds wove in and out of the mêlée; there was all the gaiety and anticipation of the moments before a hunt sets off. I could hear cries, laughter, the baying of dogs and noted in the jostling throng, the groom holding my horse and gazing questioningly in my direction.

Cordelia, who was mounted (to follow, not to hunt), nudged her chestnut through the crush and rode close to the windows, also, mutely, asking me when I would emerge. I gestured to her with the letter and indicated I would not be long. An unconfident rider, she turned her horse and urged it through to where it was less crowded.

Now that I had begun to read this letter, though every line pointed towards an alarming conclusion, I thought that I had better finish it for good or ill. As I read on I heard the horn begin to blow, the hounds go off at full cry and the thud of hooves galloping away. I pictured the hunt streaming off over the grass towards the fields beyond. They had found a scent quickly, as I had believed they might, for only the night before, leaning from my window, I had seen a pair of foxes playing on the grass outside the house. I had told no one of this, thinking to give them a chance – I am great for the chase but not for the kill, as many are, would they but confess it. As the sounds grew fainter I stood alone in the room, continuing to read Wheeler's letter, which went on:

'*Some fifteen minutes after I had commenced my efforts to induce a trance in Miss Clementi, I believe I had worn down her resistance for, though she herself was not aware of it, as I continued to swing the crystal, her eyelids began to droop – the two against the wall, I am forced to say, continuing their racket as if they were at an inn. Ere long Miss Clementi became lethargic, I took her two hands in mine, her eyes opened, then closed again. She was at last in a trance.*

'*Mr Mortimer and his companion, observing some*

change in the situation, now stopped their banter and came closer. I then commanded Miss Clementi to open her eyes. She did. She was under my influence at last.

'I began by asking her a few trifling questions, to which she did not respond in any way. I then said, "Maria – you know you can speak. And now you must speak. Speak now." She did not, but I observed her head twitching a little, as if in agitation, and that she breathed faster. The two men were now all attention. I knew I must proceed slowly and with care. I recognised Miss Clementi was an imperfect subject for mesmerism. She was one of those rare persons who, even in a trance, retain some final controls. And I recognised it was my reference to her inability to speak which caused her such agitation.

'Mr Goodall – on one occasion long ago I continued to demand answers to questions which disturbed my subject rather as I was now disturbing Miss Clementi. I will not describe the consequences but they were very grave and I vowed I would never do such a thing again. But I had witnesses urging me on as if they were at a cockfight; I had the most intense curiosity to get to the heart of this intriguing mystery. I took a risk I should not have taken and repeated my words to her, telling her that she could speak and must speak. Alas, her agitation increased. She began to toss her head from side to side with the very motion of a woman trying to keep strangling hands from her neck. Her chest rose and fell convulsively as if she were about to go into a frenzy. And still she made no sound.

'Then her mouth opened. She screamed. She cried, "The fire! I'm burning! The fire!" Then she screamed

again, then began twisting in her chair as if in great pain, as if, veritably, burning.

'*I reached forward, took her by the shoulders, put my face to hers and was about to demand that she woke, for the pain she was in seemed terrible, when her body suddenly relaxed and she began, my face still close to hers, but completely unaware of my presence, to sing, in French, in a childish voice – by no means that of the Maria Clementi we have heard on the stage. What she sang was that odious ditty of the French revolutionaries, the Ça ira, which they sang as they advanced through the streets and countryside of France to kill and loot their fellow countrymen. Though that song is half a century old now, it still represents that spirit of frenzied rebellion which brings a shudder to all who remember the past – or fear the future. "Ça ira, ça ira, ça ira . . ." she sang, but as if – to me, it seemed – she had learned it as a child at her mother's or father's knee. Not such a strange idea, I suppose, for nothing is known of her past. Perhaps her parents had worn the red bonnet of the Revolution.*

'*By this time Mr Mortimer and his nameless companion had become much alarmed. It is one thing to witness a demonstration where a man mimics animals or a lady holds her arm above her head without apparent pain or discomfort for five minutes: it is another to see a young woman mesmerised and brought to the portals of the madhouse. And this was, alas, what I had brought about.*

'*The young nobleman, for so I judged him to be, stood there, mouth agape, half-horrified and half-fascinated, and there was that in his manner which unhappily reminded me of a visitor in a brothel, a man watching a display in a whorehouse. Mortimer, a man of some sense, whatever his moral character, acted to stop the matter, though misguidedly, and rushed forward, attempting to lay hands on Miss Clementi, crying as he did so, "Maria! Maria! Wake up, for God's sake!"*

'I, still having hold of Miss Clementi's shoulders, shook my head violently and hissed at him, "No — let me do this. You may harm her." Whereupon he retreated a pace and I roused Miss Clementi with one calm order that she should awake and forget all that had occurred during her trance condition. She ceased to sing, opened her eyes and gazed quite calmly at all of us, seeming unaware of what had taken place during the preceding minutes. Then she rose to her feet, looked round at our astonished faces and left the room with a graceful tread. With difficulty I prevented Mortimer and his friend from following. I rang for a servant and sent her to her mistress, whom she reported, only minutes later, to be lying on her bed fully dressed but for her shoes, in a profound sleep.

'"But will she speak when she wakes?" was Mortimer's urgent question. I could not know and told him this. I warned him not to inform her of what had befallen her while in her trance, for I feared to recall to her conscious mind that which had so disturbed her.

'Since that afternoon I have met with Mortimer, who tells me that when Miss Clementi awoke from her sleep some hours later and in time for her evening's performance, she was mute as ever. Mortimer had obeyed my instructions and told her little of what had passed that afternoon though she had been curious, inasmuch as she was able to express that curiosity. Miss Clementi,

he told me, wished to proceed with the attempt to regain or restore her powers of speech. I responded by saying I was most reluctant to try again soon, particularly, I stressed to him, in the undesirable atmosphere he and his friend had created on the previous occasion. Emphatically, I told him, it had been obvious to me, as it must have been to him, that Miss Clementi was able to speak, for she had done so when she cried out 'Fire! I'm burning!' in such a harrowing manner.

'But I told him I considered her affliction to be such as I had met before, though seldom, where my subject appeared to be obeying unheard orders to behave in a particular manner. I told Mortimer I had caused cripples to walk and stammerers to cease stammering. But always my impression had been that the condition was imposed on the sufferer by orders given to that individual by himself *which he dared not disobey until in a mesmeric trance, when I countermanded the order he had given to himself. Did Mortimer, I asked, know of Miss Clementi's having been in a fire where she lost those she loved — had perhaps not raised the alarm in time, and therefore sentenced herself to perpetual silence?*

'Mortimer said he knew nothing of such an event and, to put it bluntly, seemed to dismiss all I said as rubbish. His proposition was that while mesmerised some imaginings of Miss Clementi's had been released and that they were not to be taken seriously. The important thing, he claimed, was that while under my influence she had spoken, and therefore the sooner she and I met again to continue the work, the better. He had no doubt that in a week or two she would speak.

I told him that, while under mesmeric power subjects were not dreaming, as he seemed to imagine, but were less given to fancy and imagination than most of us are in our day-to-day lives.

'He ignored everything I said; there was no reasoning with him. I believe he is partly altruistic in wishing to get Miss Clementi to speak, but it cannot be ignored that he sees profit ahead not only for the lady but more for himself if she could take speaking parts. I have told him bluntly that I hesitate to proceed, fearing for Miss Clementi's sanity, as much as anything else – and certainly would not contemplate seeing her in the pothouse atmosphere he and his friend had created on the previous occasion. Were I to attempt again, I told him, I would need the support of a doctor and some respectable female friend of Miss Clementi's. Her reaction, I told him, had been as unusual and as horrifying as anything I had seen in thirty years and I would not answer for the consequences if some reckless and ill-thought-out attempt to restore her voice were made.

'I confess to you, Mr Goodall, that only these considerations prevent my recommencing the work immediately. For I am immensely curious about the case of Miss Clementi, which might advance our knowledge of mesmerism considerably. But science has its responsibilities. A man yearning to learn more of medicine may dissect a hundred corpses without harming any living thing and the results of his dissections may be beneficial to future generations. But where the subject is alive a man in pursuit of knowledge must take his responsibilities seriously. Knowledge must not be gained

*at the expense of the health and happiness of another –
yet, alas, Mr Goodall, a man will always be tempted –
always.*

'*To conclude, I parted on bad terms with Mortimer.
He wrote me an hour later, full of apologies, and since
then I have received a letter daily from him, urging
me to visit Miss Clementi again and use my powers
of mesmerism on her. He has offered me a large sum
of money, which I have refused. He is now recruiting
others to his cause and I fear the pressures on me will
mount.*

'*In short, my dear Mr Goodall, I appeal to you to
favour me with your thoughts and advice about what
should be done. Miss Clementi has no family and
appears to have no true friends about her, though
there are many, I think, who wish to exploit her.
Can you help or can you direct me to someone else
who might provide me with guidance? I keenly await
your reply.*'

I cursed as I put down the letter. Yet even as I cursed,
I wondered what should I do? I was tempted to go to
London, from a curiosity I knew I should restrain and
because, I argued, it was I who had set this affair in
motion, therefore I owed it to myself to see it through.
In my mind's eye I saw Maria writhing in her chair,
afflicted by visions, even the very sensation of fire. But,
great gods! – what would my family think? I had come
here with my bride-to-be and would be abandoning her
after less than a week. What would Cordelia think of
me for leaving her with my family, whom she had only
just met, to go off to London and involve myself again
in this murky affair? No, I declared to myself, I could

not go, would not go, did not wish to go. I would write a judicious letter to Wheeler that very night. I would not go to London.

With that thought I left the room rapidly and found my groom back in the stable yard, walking my horse up and down. I got up on my good old Rodney and off I went.

A good gallop across open fields chasing the sound of the hunting horn blew away thoughts of Wheeler's letter. Soon I was up to the infantry, then caught up with the riders, passing Flora, spurring on her little mount, with Cordelia riding soberly beside her. Galloping on over a little rise, I found the hunt streaming across a vast ploughed field under a sky of clear pale blue. Ahead of them, plunging for the cover of a hedge, I detected the darting fox.

We crossed another field and headed at a gallop through our own coalfields, the horses' hooves drumming on the hard-packed earth as we passed the winches carrying swaying buckets to the surface, a group of black-faced men, a small group of drably dressed women sorting coal in vast troughs. Once through these two acres of blackened earth and puddles we were back in fields and it was in a copse at the end of one that the hounds finally caught up with our quarry and it was over. But no sooner had we clustered round the kill than some of the dogs caught another scent and we were off again, over hill and dale. We killed twice that day and would have gone on, but then down came the rain, drenching horses, men and hounds and the scent, too; so we turned for home, well satisfied, arriving weary, soaked, but in excellent heart.

Later, by the drawing-room fire we sat comfortable again. My sisters, Cordelia and Mrs Frazer were sewing for dear life: there was to be a ball at a neighbour's house in three days' time, so that many hems were being raised and lowered, ribbons being replaced and necklaces rethreaded. My father was in his study, though Arabella's betrothed was with us, handing thimbles and the like. I sat to one side, watching the rain pour down over the window panes and over the flat landscape, and began to think anew of Wheeler's letter.

Cordelia might have read those thoughts for she raised her head from her sewing and asked. 'What was the burden of this morning's letter to you, Jonathan?'

'It was from Mr Wheeler, the mesmerist,' I responded. This caused much interest, of course. On the way down from London Cordelia, Mrs Frazer and I had agreed to spare the Kittering folk as much as possible of the horrid story of Frankenstein, though the news of his attack, so shortly after the murder of his wife and child, was of course known. Now I told the company, 'Miss Maria Clementi, the singer, whom you may know is able to sing but is otherwise completely mute, was present at the time of the attack on my friend Victor Frankenstein. Many doctors have tried to restore her power of speech and failed, so as a last resort it was thought a mesmerist should be asked if he could help her. Thus she might be able to tell us what she saw when Mr Frankenstein was attacked.'

'Dangerous games,' Dudley Hight observed from his chair – predictably, perhaps. Stout-hearted squire that he was, he was more concerned with his land and the doings in the locality than the strange affairs of the city.

'Well, then,' said Cordelia. 'Did he report on a meeting between himself and Miss Clementi? What was the outcome?'

I left the window and went to sit with the party by the fire. I was not altogether happy about speaking. Flora was among us, frowning over her cross-stitch, and I am not one who thinks it a duty to present children with unpleasant facts at an early age in order to harden them. I had decided earlier not to go to London but to write instead to Wheeler. Yet I now began to recognise I was tempted as a man recognises he has a sickness in the blood.

I said only, 'The outcome was not a good one. Wheeler believes he will make no further attempts to discover Miss Clementi's voice,' and that, in spite of many curious questions, was all I said.

That night I wrote to Wheeler advising him to visit Maria no more. I would see him, I said, when I came next to London.

The rain poured down next day and the next, but the morning after that dawned fresh and blue. In the evening there would be a ball at a neighbour's to which even I looked forward. I rose early and was about to set out to our coalfields for an early interview with the overseer there when a maid came with a letter into the stable yard, where I was waiting for my horse to be saddled. With sinking heart I recognised that flourishing, ornate hand and the pale blue ink. I had resisted going to London. What fresh horrors had Wheeler to impart from a distance? Any faint hope I had that the news might be reassuring was destroyed as soon as I read the opening sentences:

'Mr Goodall – I expect you will by now have received my last letter in which I told you I feared to go further with Miss Clementi. I mentioned also that I had warned Mr Mortimer it might be dangerous to do so, but, alas, far from heeding my advice he has ignored it completely and has embarked on a course which alarms me greatly. Events move fast. I need your advice and, perhaps, practical help in the matter.

'Mr Mortimer and his associate, the young man of whom I told you – it appears he is Mr John Nottcutt, nephew of the Duke of North Shields (and the biggest libertine at large, in my opinion and that of many others) – have hatched a plot together. They have arranged for March 4th a demonstration of mesmerism with Miss Clementi at the Royal Society in front of a host of invited dignitaries, both scientists and other notables. I have said over and over I dread going on with Miss Clementi without good safeguards. Now – imagine my horror of proceeding without such safeguards and before a large audience of people.

'You might say, Mr Goodall – then Wheeler, do not do so. But consider my position as sympathetically as you can, I beg you. I am a man without means other than what I can earn by my powers. I depend on the favour of others. Mr Nottcutt is the eldest son of the brother of a Duke. The Duke himself is in poor health. If I refuse I run the risk of earning the enmity of the future head of one of the most powerful families in the land (and Mr Nottcutt, let us be clear, is not one to take lightly the smallest slight). I live by the patronage of such men. I fear to offend them, I much need now the counsel and perhaps the support of a gentleman such as yourself,

more able than I am to engage with Mr Nottcutt on equal
terms, more capable, to put it bluntly, of taking the force
of his wrath and weathering it.

'*I assure you I am more upset than I can say in*
addressing you so soon again, and particularly in these
terms, but I fear for Miss Clementi and for myself if
the plan devised by Mortimer and Mr Nottcutt goes
ahead.'

The brightness left the day as I finished reading this
letter. I rode out across fields to the coalfields in a
miserable frame of mind. I saw some men, women and
children plodding off to their work. These dark-visaged
people in their work-blackened clothes depressed my
spirits even further.

I would have welcomed any letter from Wheeler
removing the temptation to go off to London. This,
however, removed any excuse to stay away – it was
I who bore most of the responsibility for the terrible
outcome of an attempt to get Maria to speak.

That graceless fellow Gabriel Mortimer and his
strange ally, John Nottcutt, proposed to put Maria
on public exhibition, like a freak at a fair. Mortimer
obviously felt that this would increase her – and his –
fame; Nottcutt, I suppose, was moved by idle curiosity,
as a boy pokes an anthill with a stick to see the insects
run about. And Wheeler had earned himself many a
guinea by his association with the powerful, a living,
understandably enough, he did not wish to endanger.
All of which left poor Maria Clementi being moved by
a villain, a knave and a poltroon.

I had been away from the febrile excitement, the
terrors, the mysteries of the situation surrounding Victor

Frankenstein for one week – and already I was being drawn irresistibly back. No help for it – if I was going next day I must impart the news immediately to my family – and to Cordelia. This I did. It would be for days only, I told them, then I would return at speed. Faces were pulled, pity was expressed that I found myself forced to go again to London. Into Cordelia's eyes I could not look. She spoke to me little during the day.

It was that evening, as I dressed for the ball, she came to my bedroom and sat unceremoniously on my bed, watching me put on my tailcoat. She said, 'Jonathan – must you return to London? Can it not wait? Can it not go on without you at all?'

'I fear I must go, dear,' said I, feeling a hypocrite and growing angry as a man will.

'Are you bored here in the country?' she asked.

'My dear Cordelia. This is my home where those I hold dearest in the world are all gathered together. I assure you, I leave because I feel I must, not because I wish to.' Yet I knew as I spoke that my desire to pry into all the corners of the world was leading me from home, a man of my disposition would leave Heaven itself to see what mesmeric power could make of Maria Clementi. I would choose differently now, but then I was young and eager, lured against my will, by Maria. I had not discovered into what danger the lust to know may take a man.

Cordelia stood up to retie my cravat for me and said, as she did so, 'I fear for you, Jonathan. It is not only that the murderer is at large, and is close to those he is persecuting, though that is bad enough: it is that I sense something the Scotch would call 'uncanny'. It makes me shudder. It has done so from the start, and now it grows worse. Can you wonder I am afraid for you?'

Then I took her in my arms and will say no more of what followed. I was misled by vanity again, believing the main reason for her disliking my visit to London was her fear of Miss Clementi's charms. And – my Cordelia's instincts have ever been true – her battle too was with the demon of curiosity within me, that devilish heretical impulse to *know*.

As we went downstairs to take a little tea and bread and butter before the ball I told her, 'My greatest comfort is that you and Flora will be here in safety with my family, who have already taken you to their hearts.'

'It is sad I shall not feel as comfortable about you,' was all she replied – reducing my ease considerably. In short, making me feel a villain.

Meanwhile we took our tea. My father had been persuaded to accompany us to the dancing and had put on his old bottle-green coat, always pulled out for such occasions. As Arabella and Anna often disrespectfully remarked, this garment might have made its first bow at the court of Queen Anne. The ladies went off to take last looks in their glasses, leaving my father and myself alone at the table among the tea-cups. We had settled for a stiffening glass of claret apiece when he said to me, quite harshly, 'I hear you leave us tomorrow, Jonathan. I do not understand you. I'm given to believe you'll ride a hundred miles in all weathers to witness an experiment in mesmerism, leaving behind you, after only a few days, the charming woman you wish to make your wife. I had counted on you to be here, sir, to assist in the business of the estate. More important, Mrs Downey needs you here. I believe you're mad.'

'Well, I think I must go, father,' I said.

'I hope you don't plan to fall in love with this foreign dancer,' he said, cutting to the heart of the matter. 'A dumb beauty may have much appeal for a man but I pray you'll resist. I have long hoped for your marriage and the arrival of the admirable Cordelia Downey rejoiced my heart. No better woman could have been found, had she had ten thousand pounds a year. I fear she will take your defection as a rejection of her, which she does not deserve. I would much dislike to see anything go amiss with the marriage.'

'It will not,' I assured him, in no very good temper, for I half lied, but would not admit it, and that makes a man angry. And my father believed what I said, and that made it all the worse.

The ball took place and I will not describe the candles, the dresses or the music, though I fancied my Cordelia just a little distant with me, nor was I encouraged when I saw her lightly tripping over the floor in a polka and then in a cotillion with the local cavaliers. It was a mercy in our backward part of the country the waltz was still considered less than decent at that time, for had I seen her whirling in the close embrace of others, I might have burst my buttons. Even so, the sight of Cordelia dancing gaily with others at all did not cheer me. Gloom is always our attendant as we embark on a voyage for dubious reasons.

Next day I left the house before anyone was up.

I was in London by afternoon, muddied from head to toe and the horse near dropping. Horse stabled, I went straight to Wheeler's lodgings in Farringdon Road where his landlady told me sullenly he was gone – had packed a valise and been driven off to Grosvenor Square in a coach with a coat of arms painted on the side. On I went to Russell Square to find Maria and was there told she was visiting at Nottcutt House, in Grosvenor Square. So that was where the cast of the play was assembling, thought I, and off I too went to Grosvenor Square, to one of the handsome new mansions there, houses of unprecedented splendour. The door was opened to me by a footman in livery who looked askance at my travel-stained clothes.

By using the name of Mr Nottcutt, I achieved an entrance into the large marble hall hung with pictures, where a great fire burned in a marble fireplace and a porter snoozed in a red leather armchair. This hall was large enough to absorb a whole floor of Mrs Downey's house and still leave room to hang the laundry. The sight of such wealth helped me to understand more fully Wheeler's fear of a quarrel with its possessors.

A butler with more presence than a prime minister claimed me and led me up a sweeping marble staircase, then along lofty carpeted corridors, under candle-holders burning with lights, to a door, where the butler knocked – and knocked again. After a pause this door was opened a crack, in a furtive manner hardly consistent with the dignity of the house. The face in the doorway was that of Augustus Wheeler. His look when he saw me was cautious, almost suspicious. He made no move to open the door further. As the recipient of two letters from him imploring my intervention I had thought he would hail me as a saviour. It appeared this was not to be the case.

'Let me in, Wheeler?' I asked, though he had no right to deny me. Reluctantly it seemed, he opened up further and I stepped in. He shut the door quickly behind me.

This must have been one of the smaller rooms in the house, though it was twenty feet square. It was handsomely furnished in blue and gilt with a beautiful and no doubt costly Chinese carpet upon the floor and a gilt mirror from France over the fireplace. The individuals in the room did not match its style.

On a *chaise-longue* opposite the fire, in the centre of the room, lay Maria Clementi in a loose blue robe in Arabic style, her hair undone and falling over her shoulders. She was pale, appearing lethargic, even exhausted, though just as beautiful as ever. Gabriel Mortimer lay negligently in a chair wearing his burgundy coat and trousers, one gleaming boot propped up on a stool. His curls shone no less glossily, his watch-chain was no smaller than before. The black eyes of his ruined face were on Maria; he barely glanced at me as I came in.

Standing by the fireplace was a tall, dandified figure in a smoking-coat of dark red velvet, whom I assumed was Mr Nottcutt. This gentleman's hair and moustache were yellow as butter, his face long, pale and inexpressive and his mouth rather small and slack. One glance at John Nottcutt and I knew him and disliked what I saw. Here was a man whose wealth and position had from his earliest years supplied him with everything but that which may ultimately be of most value to us, the close and loving attention of parents, friends and kinsfolk, often as hard to come by in the houses of the wealthy as in the overcrowded hovels of the poor. Reared by the basest servants, introduced to every indulgence at an early age by those who had not the power to restrain him, trained neither to work nor think nor to exercise self-control, Nottcutt was an empty man. Boredom was an ever-lurking enemy, one to be defeated at all costs and by all means. Meanwhile, he loved my appearance as much as much as I loved his. He gave me and my bespattered clothing a smile of amusement, intended to insult.

Wheeler, having let me in, moved rapidly across the room to the thickly curtained windows and sat down close by them as if attempting to conceal himself in their folds.

About the room stood plates and dishes, relics of an old meal, or several. On a Chinese chest stood wine bottles and a flask of yellowish liquid I took to be laudanum. The air was heavy with smoke. One would have sworn from the postures of those present that no one and nothing in the room had moved for hours. It was as though the sun stood still; time had ceased.

Meanwhile, no one spoke to greet me, to introduce me to Mr Nottcutt, or to invite me to be seated. I was obliged, still standing by the door like a servant come for orders, to break the uncomfortable silence myself, saying across the room to Augustus Wheeler, 'Mr Wheeler – alarmed by your recent letters I have hastened here from Nottingham. I apologise for arriving still in my travelling clothes, but I felt from your tone it was a matter of urgency. I must ask you gentlemen whether it is right to put Miss Clementi on public show at the

Royal Society. Do you think her nerves will stand this, after what you saw at the last encounter?' (I wondered whether Maria's *belle indifference* had come from the laudanum flask.)

Nottcutt, at the fireplace, looked me up and down and asked insolently. 'Who are you? What right have you to interfere?'

Mortimer hastily introduced me to him, but did not supply his name to me, treating me as if I had come in with coals for the fire. This made me love neither of them better I must tell you. Mortimer, stating my name, called Nottcutt 'Sandor', and I thought 'Sandor'? What sort of a name is that, and what jiggery-pokery is occurring here?

The atmosphere in the room was so strange and so private and the air of those in the room so like a conspiracy that I felt as if I were in a coven of witches and warlocks. However, I was forced to blunder on, addressing Maria, saying, 'Miss Clementi – has anyone spoken to you of the distress you endured while in your trance? Did they tell you that you cried out "Fire!", then contorted yourself as if you were burning? Has the gentleman I see over there in his corner, as if planning to disappear into the wall, mentioned to you that he has written to me twice in one week, saying he feared for you if you undertook more experiments like the first, are you not concerned that you will be helpless on a stage before a large crowd of men and women? Think, Miss Clementi, think, I beg you, what you are doing.'

My vehemence was wasted. To the earlier questions she gave an indifferent nod, to the rest she raised a shoulder where she lay, as if in a shrug. I despaired

for her – and of her. I felt also much at a disadvantage
and very angry with Wheeler, who had called me here,
and now took no part in the conversation, afraid, no
doubt, of Nottcutt's displeasure.

'Wheeler!' I cried out to him. 'Will you risk this
woman's health, risk her possible humiliation in a most
public manner?'

He gazed at me for a second, then turned his eyes to
Gabriel Mortimer, who was frowning slightly. None in
that room, neither the lounging men, nor the reclining
woman, moved. Nottcutt now regarded me steadily
with some menace behind his stare. It would not be
long before he summoned a servant to escort me out.
Thinking to avoid the final shame of being conducted
from the house at his orders, I took my leave, to the
perfect indifference of all there.

As I left I said, 'I shall go to Sir Humphry, President
of the Royal Society, and put my case; tell him I believe
this performance, for so it is, ought to be cancelled.'

'You may do as you please,' mumbled Nottcutt, as
if obliged to comment on the weather.

I left that room feeling thoroughly foolish, put out
and angry. Wheeler, who had brought me to London to
defend him against the others, was now their accomplice
– even Maria, for whatever reason, was prepared to
perform. Had she been intimidated, drugged, or was it
from vanity? I could not guess.

Sir Humphry Davy, whom we coal-owners have reason
to bless, and to whom I had the honour of being
presented when a boy, was not in London, but I
was directed to the home of another officer of the

esteemed Society whom I was assured would be able to assist me.

This gentleman, Mr Plomer, alas, told me much what I expected, that many invitations had gone out and been accepted, some by those living at a distance. It would be impossible to inform all these guests in time that Wheeler's demonstration had been cancelled. I then informed him of what I had not said earlier, that it was believed Miss Clementi knew details of the horrible attack on Mr Frankenstein and that this evidence had been one of the reasons for embarking on the attempt to restore her powers of speech. If, I stated, she were to blurt all that information forth in public, it would be very disagreeable for any ladies present and certainly a most undesirable way for evidence against a vile criminal to be presented. He shook his head at this, uttering that most discouraging of phrases, 'I wish I had known this earlier.'

Science is a ruthless mistress. She can put a fever in the blood. For her sake a man can disregard all the laws of God and man as a man may gamble away his estates and ruin his family to satisfy a mistress's whims. However, propriety is also a stern mistress. I pointed out that I found it quite indecent that Miss Clementi, a young woman, should be embarking on this ordeal, as it might prove to be, in front of a large audience without a single person, still less one of her own sex, to support her. This gave him pause.

Plomer, alarmed now, declared, 'Goodall, I do not know if you are right or wrong in your suspicions of Mr Wheeler's demonstrations – let us hope you are wrong – but the invitations are out and, alas, it is too late to withdraw them. So that is that. Nevertheless, it is quite undesirable for Miss Clementi to have with her no suitable attendant. Will you find one?'

To this I agreed.

I returned to Gray's Inn Road, suspecting Sir Humphry might have done better for me than Plomer. I reflected that had those invited to the demonstration – performance, rather – been colliers and washerwomen rather than the luminaries of the land, a stop might have been put to the proceedings. But there was no help for it now. The demonstration would take place unless some other means could be found of preventing it.

Much fatigued by now, I got to the house, where my arrival much disconcerted the servants, who were enjoying the absence of the family. I sat down and penned a letter to Mrs Jacoby, whose address in Chatham my clever Cordelia had thought to obtain before the lady left for the cold home of her sister. In it I begged her to forget the pains of the past and come once again, and for the last time, to the aid of her former employer. I feared, I said, Miss Clementi had fallen utterly into the wrong hands. I told her of the unholy alliance of Wheeler, Mortimer and Nottcutt and of the way Miss Clementi, while in a trance, had called out about fire. Now this dangerous experiment was about to be repeated in public. Would she, I asked, take a chaise from Chatham at my expense and come at all speed to London?

I was not sure my appeal would succeed. Mrs Jacoby might be absent from home and even if she received my letter in time I thought she might stick to her guns and refuse to have any more dealings with Maria.

Nevertheless, I sent off my message by the fastest means possible, hoping Mrs Jacoby would come to my assistance in time.

The upper part of the house was in the process of thorough cleaning and very cold, no fires having been lit there for days, so I told the servants I would make do in the parlour. I had a fire lit there, stripped off my muddy clothes, arranged for food and hot water to be brought and generally set up an encampment.

Early that evening I went to that mournful house at Cheyne Walk which had been rendered a little more hospitable by the arrival of Victor's parents. The two guards, however, still occupied the drawing-room.

Mrs Frankenstein was a tall, handsome woman, though evidently worn by caring for her son, still, she said, gravely ill. She greeted me kindly and took me into a little room downstairs which she had taken over for herself. She described to me how she had been forced to stop the visits of Miss Clementi to Victor, who, on one occasion, had found the strength to whisper, 'Mother. She is killing me.' Of course she asked me about the relations of her son and Maria Clementi but I could scarcely tell her of the wicked passion for the actress Victor had conceived, even before his wife's cruel murder. I felt, however, that I must describe the efforts being made to bring back Maria's power of speech, and the hope that she would be able to give evidence about Victor's attacker. Mrs Frankenstein expressed keen interest in this and asked me whether she and Mr Frankenstein might attend the Royal Society demonstration. I offered to write then and there to request that seats be made available to them. The message was taken off by a servant.

It was then that Victor's mother told me something which astonished and disturbed me, speaking of the matter as if she assumed I was familiar with it. 'He is much afflicted by the death of his wife and child,' she told me, 'and I fear his recovery is much impeded by grief. And sometimes in delirium, he murmurs of his first wife, his loved step-sister, of course, with whom he grew up.'

I could not conceal my expression of astonishment at her words. Victor had not told me he had been married before. Mrs Frankenstein noted my surprise before I had a chance to hide it and asked me, 'You did not know of Victor's first wife, Elizabeth Lavengro?'

'I do not know. I forgot, perhaps,' was my very inadequate response. It seemed very strange Victor had not mentioned an earlier marriage.

Mrs Frankenstein looked at me in some puzzlement, unable to credit a man could entirely forget the marriage of a friend, or this is what I thought. Alas, what she said next was far more alarming. 'Poor Victor. What unlucky stars must have been in the heavens at his moment of birth. How could a man bear two such great afflictions? How could any man recover from two bereavements such as he has sustained – two wives, both murdered?'

Both murdered, she said. My head reeled. I felt I was taking leave of my senses and must indeed have looked very odd, for Mrs Frankenstein bent towards me and asked if I felt ill, and indeed I did. I could not face a visit to the sick man upstairs, knowing what he had kept from me, from all of us and so, left the house.

I made my way somehow back to Gray's Inn Road, flung myself in an armchair with a bottle of brandy by my side and spent the remainder of the evening brooding over what Victor's mother had innocently revealed. The universe was spinning round me, not at first due to the brandy (though perhaps later). Then, wearily undressing, I fell into a deep, fuddled sleep, my last thought being only what my first had been on hearing Mrs Frankenstein's words. How could a man, a friend, have kept back from others all information about a first marriage, ending cruelly in murder? He might refrain at first, unable to speak of the pain of the event – but surely he would inevitably refer to it when a second wife was killed? Not to do so was unnatural. Unless – it was an unworthy thought, but most men would have thought it – he had himself been responsible for both crimes.

It was only thanks to the long gallop to London and my business during the afternoon – as well as to the brandy, I suppose – that I managed to sleep that night. I was in fact awoken late in the morning by the arrival of Mrs Jacoby, who had received my message the previous day and set out at dawn from Chatham.

She came in bundled up in many layers of clothing and deeply chilled. Over a glass of mulled wine she told me, 'I wish to God I were not here, Mr Goodall. I never slept a wink last night. I have a premonition of disaster. Something dreadful will occur, I'm certain of it. I would not have come, but for knowing I have helped to create this situation, and I feel it is a duty to see how it comes out and help to relieve myself of guilt.' At this she flung up her arms and cried out, 'Oh, Lord! Oh, my good Lord! I have collaborated with sin, Oh Lord, Lord! Hear me and forgive. I have been a handmaiden to Satan, Lord. Forgive me, forgive me!'

I gazed at this exhibition with some horror. I was not then, and still am not, a believer in public rantings, weepings and declarations of faith. These days I may be a little more sedulous in my religious duties but I have as little taste for all that now as I had then. When Mrs Jacoby had left Maria Clementi's service she had stated she felt she had much to atone for, but this remorse, in the hands of her nonconformist sister, had flourished and thrown out exotic blooms. I could not help preferring the old unreclaimed Mrs Jacoby and was uncertain how useful she would be in her new form when it came to dealing with a world far from the chapels of Chatham. All I felt able to say was, 'Take more hot wine, Mrs Jacoby. Our breakfast will soon be here.'

She looked at me severely, saying, 'Call on your Maker, Mr Goodall. You, I and Maria Clementi – all need His help. Are you a true believer?'

Still preoccupied with my extraordinary suspicions of Frankenstein, and anxious about the day ahead, I responded to this bluntly, 'I asked you to come here, Mrs Jacoby, and am happy you have done so, but let me be frank, if you are to keep calling on your Maker and putting into His hands what should rightly be in your own, I would prefer to send you straight back to Chatham.'

This sobered her a little. 'I will help you, of course.' she said. 'Yet I dread what is to come.'

'Then you had better eat and take some rest for we must be ready for action,' I said as the food came in. The soldier's widow saw the point of this advice. I was cheered to hear her say, 'From your letter I concluded it would be best if Maria did not take part in this demonstration at all. I propose to go and see her and shall try to get her alone and dissuade her from appearing. Do you know where she is to be found?'

I told her Maria had cancelled her theatrical performances, so would be away from the theatre but most probably at Russell Square or Nottcutt House in Grosvenor Square.

'Very well, then,' said the good woman. 'I shall try to find her at one of those addresses and prevent this ungodly show.' And after taking a rapid meal she called on her Maker a little more, then collected herself together and left the house in military style.

I repaired to the Voyagers' Club and over coffee read the newspapers. Wheeler's coming demonstration at the Royal Society was announced, to my gloom. I earnestly hoped Mrs Jacoby would succeed in persuading Maria to withdraw from the event. If she could not, it would go ahead, and God knew what the result would be. At least, I thought, at the end of the day it would be over, for good or ill, and I on my way back to Nottingham. Whatever the outcome I must not let this affair detain me in London. If I did, I knew Cordelia would cease to believe in me and my promises. She loved me. I was sure of it. But she was a proud and high-spirited woman and would not take insult from me. It would seem her late husband had not been the easiest of men. She was wary of marrying another husband like the first and might well

take the view that a man who cannot behave himself
during the courtship would be unlikely to improve later.
And what would I do, I thought, if she believed I stayed
in London because I was entranced by Maria Clementi?
What would my future be if Cordelia rejected me, if I
lost her while stranded in this melancholy, mysterious
world, this dark side of the moon?

When I returned to the house Mrs Jacoby had already
returned. Her search for Maria had been futile. She had
been told at Russell Square that Maria had not been
there for some days. Enquiring for her at Nottcutt House
she heard that Mr Nottcutt and a party of friends had left
for another of his residences at Richmond and would not
come back until much later in the day. There was hardly
time, before the demonstration, to go to Richmond on
the chance that Maria was still there. I guessed Maria
had been deliberately hidden away from other influences
until the time came for the demonstration at the Royal
Society. I hoped at least they had rehearsed her there,
to make certain nothing untoward would occur during
the demonstration. But in the event, that, alas, was
not to be.

FIFTEEN

On the afternoon of the demonstration it was dark; in the great hall at the Royal Society many candles glowed in the chandeliers, casting light on the dignified and fashionable assembly. I arrived in good time with Mrs Jacoby, but even so we had to force our way to the front of the hall through a chattering crowd standing or seated on narrow, fragile chairs. Further off was a platform with two seats. We had earlier called at Nottcutt House in a last attempt to talk to Maria, but were told that the Richmond party had not returned. We now found ourselves part of the vast audience which comprised grey-bearded dignitaries, ladies in silks with fans, politicians, fops, professors, men and women of great rank and position. There, too, seated quietly together, were Victor's parents, Mr and Mrs Frankenstein. As we reached the front Mrs Jacoby indicated another couple, sitting in the front row of chairs, 'Those are Nottcutt's parents in front. They are quiet country dwellers. I should not have expected to find them here.'

'Let us hope that nothing in this charade will upset their quiet rural temper,' I responded.

There was an upholstered settle to the side of the room and on it we found Maria Clementi seated, simply attired in a cream dress and mantle, a small low-crowned bonnet on her head. Beside her sat Augustus Wheeler, severely dressed in a dark coat and trousers. Nottcutt leaned against the wall beside Maria and in front of the pair on the settle stood Gabriel Mortimer, a little soberer in his attire than usual, but, when he turned to greet, or rather, confront me, I saw a large diamond pin, big as a pea, in his cravat. Outside this inner circle were others, orbiting Maria's planet as it seemed, all trying to beg a word, seize a glance, find out in advance what was to be the nature of the event to come – a politer version of the kind of shoving and crowding which takes place among the French when a man or woman of notoriety is present.

Mrs Jacoby and I determinedly achieved the settle, where an eminent man of science was bent over Wheeler in conversation. Two ladies in silks and Indian shawls leaned talking towards Maria, who stared ahead of her not acknowledging their presence in any way, this being tolerable to them, I suppose, merely because she was known to be mute. Wheeler spotted me, though he did not, at that point, observe Mrs Jacoby, who stood slightly behind me. Seeing me, Wheeler looked shocked and broke off his talk with the eminent man. He stood up abruptly, evidently attracting the attention of Gabriel Mortimer, for he swung round, by which time both I and

Mrs Jacoby were up to them. The ladies near Maria also straightened and turned to hear Mortimer saying angrily to me, 'What are you doing here, Goodall? And you, Rebecca? You are unwelcome.'

Mrs Jacoby then said, 'To you perhaps, Gabriel. But I wish to speak to Maria.'

Mortimer said nothing more but looked at her furiously. Mrs Jacoby, somehow pushing Wheeler aside, sat down beside Maria, who barely acknowledged her. She placed a firm hand on her arm and began to speak urgently into her face.

Meanwhile, Nottcutt was still leaning against the wall. He called over, 'Ah, Mr Goodall – the muddy gentleman of yesterday, come to spoil our amusement, I see.'

I responded loudly, 'If you consider this a good way to amuse yourself, Mr Nottcutt, putting a dumb woman on show, then we have nothing to say to each other.'

This caused some consternation, even indignation, among those surrounding us. Nottcutt merely gave a condescending smile.

Mortimer then said to me, 'Goodall. I can't imagine what you're doing in this business. I take it you have dragged Mrs Jacoby back to London to be here – I hate your confounded interference.'

I would have liked to have struck him in the face and have followed this up with doing the same to Nottcutt. Instead, I bent my head to hear Mrs Jacoby's urgent whisper to Maria: 'Oh, Maria, you cannot do this. It is disreputable. Maria, through this you may hurt yourself. Have you ever had any reason to think I had not your best interests at heart? Or Mr Goodall, for that matter. We have come to persuade you not to go through with this demonstration. What will you say, in your trance? This is reckless.' But all Maria did was put her fingers to Mrs Jacoby's lips, shake her head and smile. She seemed to have very little awareness of what was going on about her.

Gabriel Mortimer was about to argue, but at this point Nottcutt walked coolly forward, took Maria's elbow and raised her up, with the intention of presenting her to his parents. No attempt was made to stop this. He looked spitefully at Mrs Jacoby as he led Maria off.

'What is she doing? What does she think?' I asked Mrs Jacoby.

She shook her head. 'She will take part in the demonstration,' she told me. 'I am sure of it. Her mind is made up and she is very strong. Yet at the same time she seems strange, unlike herself. She has not been like this before. Gabriel, have you been dosing her with something? You know she cannot tolerate soporifics or stimulants. Have you?'

Mortimer did not reply, but instead went over to Maria, who had made her curtsey to Nottcutt's parents, Lord and Lady St Elder. Wheeler followed him.

Mrs Jacoby looked up at me and sighed. I sat down beside her. 'All my efforts have failed,' I said despondently.

My companion merely gazed at the scene now taking place. Wheeler was leading Maria up the three wooden steps of the platform and there he placed her in one of the two chairs. She sat looking in front of her, perfectly composed, her arms laid along the arms of the chair. That vigour of movement she had always possessed was entirely missing.

Now Wheeler seated himself in the chair opposite Maria's, so close that their knees almost touched. The audience ceased to clatter, chatter and move about. All were now seated; a perfect silence reigned.

'If not drugged, she is ill,' muttered Mrs Jacoby beside me.

'Perhaps Wheeler has taken the precaution of putting her in a trance before they came here,' I said. 'I wonder how much of her time she has spent under his mesmeric power during the last few days?'

The performance was about to begin. The afternoon grew darker. Shadows flickered to and fro as draughts caught at the candles. The audience, grave professors, fine ladies, peers and all, watched silently. Wheeler made several passes with his crystal before Maria's eyes, indicating confidence and satisfaction throughout. As I suspected, Maria must have been brought here already mesmerised. He then asked her, gazing into her eyes, 'Maria Clementi, are you in a trance and completely under my control?' To which she answered, 'Yes,' in a clear voice.

'Have you hitherto been entirely mute?'

'Yes,' she said again. 'I could sing but I could not speak.' Her voice was light, low and very clear. There was movement, exclamation, a buzz of comment from the audience.

'Why was it that you could not speak?' he asked.

If, as I supposed, the whole performance had been thoroughly rehearsed at Richmond, to ensure all would go smoothly in front of this distinguished audience, then this was the moment when all began to go badly wrong.

From the beautiful lips of Maria Clementi came a coarse and dreadful voice, quite different from the tone in which she had spoken earlier, which bore a distinct relationship to the voice which had captured all Europe. This was deep and grating, slurred, inconsistent in tone and accent. Indeed, throughout this whole, horrible episode Maria moved from voice to voice, imitating the tones of others as if uncertain of her own, as she perhaps was – as ignorant of her voice as of the thoughts and feelings, the very identity, it represented. It was most terrible, this inconsistency, more terrible still in that one of the voices she used was undeniably that of – Victor Frankenstein.

But first she grated in that uncouth voice, awful and slurred, 'I never spoke, damn you, because I had no language – no language was given to me by my creator at my second birth, when I was brought back from death by my maker, far away on that rocky island, where the cold sea lashed the shores. So cold,' said the voice, 'so cold. May his God damn him forever.'

There was a horrified stir in the audience, uncertain now whether it was being deceived by a staged performance or presented with a madwoman. There was a babble of talk. I heard a high, nervous laugh.

Maria now stood up, turned to face the audience. Her legs were apart, her stance full of tension, her chin up. I glanced at Wheeler, still in his chair. He was disconcerted but, showman that he was, attempted to conceal his alarm. The performance was not going according to plan. He hoped, no doubt, it would right itself, or that he would be able to set it back on course again. But he could not.

'Damn him,' she said again. Then Wheeler leapt to his feet, saying, 'Lovely Maria – tell me the truth – ' but his voice was drowned by hers as she continued. This time her voice was that of a young girl, a child, and she spoke in French: 'The first I remember is light, coming from darkness into light, cold, very cold, I was very cold.' Then in English she said, in a loving tone, deep in register, alas, all too like the voice of Victor Frankenstein, 'Then I saw a dark face bending over me, the face of a lover, the face of my creator, Victor, who loved me because he made me, made me because he loved me.'

The slurred voice in which Maria had begun came again now, like that of a man in a drunken rage, 'I know what he did, the villain, he took the other he made, my dearest, my Adam, and beat him and imprisoned him, then carried him away and sent him far, far off, to a desert, alone. Yet I knew where he was – Adam, my Adam – always where he was, what pain he was in, from the moment when I opened my eyes on the island and looked into the face of my creator, I always knew where Adam was, whether near or far. Damn Frankenstein. God damn Frankenstein.'

Wheeler, now beside her, tried to interrupt. She went on, though, now cruelly mimicking the tones of Victor himself, 'I have brought you to life, my darling, and you were to be a companion and bride to my other creation, but he shall not have you. You are mine.'

A woman screamed. A man rose to his feet and cried, 'Blasphemy! What is this blasphemy?' his voice half lost amid a host of other cries. There came a woman's piercing cry, 'No!' I thought of Victor's parents sitting in the crowd hearing these hideous calumnies against their son.

I turned, saw them sitting quite still, expressions of horror on their faces. I turned then to Mrs Jacoby, who had her hand to her mouth and was muttering, 'Is it true? Can this be true?' I grasped her arm. She was like a woman stunned. 'Help me stop this,' I urged. Mortimer meanwhile was trying to pull her to her feet, understanding that Wheeler had not the presence of mind to stop the atrocity (and still Maria's words were flowing over us) and that we must, with as much decency as was left to us, get to Maria and pull her away. And all the time the horrid monologue went on.

Did she speak the truth or not? Was this the end of Maria's long silence, the moment when all her pent-up delusions broke the banks of reason and flooded over us – or was it the truth?

The audience was still astir. There were sounds of people leaving. A man's voice called out, 'Will no one stop this?' The danger was that there might be an assault on Maria, or Wheeler or both. She spoke again and this time there was no doubt in my mind that the voice was Victor's. She crooned, 'My lover, my sweetheart. I did not mean to hurt you. But you are mine, mine now, mine forever. Oh, my love, forgive me.'

'Dear God!' I exclaimed. Then I pulled at Mrs Jacoby. 'Mrs Jacoby. Stand – help me stop this!' But she did not stir. Maria's own voice, clear and carrying, now resumed.

'He beat my lover and he beat him and beat him and kept him in the cold and dark. He said I should be his, for he was my maker. I would not be his. I knew nothing, knew not myself, even, except that I did not want him. So then he took him away and put him, Adam, for many weeks and weeks in chains in a ship sailing for a far away shore. Then he was kind to me, my maker, and I turned to him for he fed me and petted me and tried to make me love him, but though I turned to him – for he was my god and said I must love and worship him yet – yet – I still yearned after my true love, the other he had created, the man he had created me for.' Then her voice became savage. 'He gave me drink. I slept. Then there was fire, much fire.' She screamed. 'Burning. Burning. The door will not open. He has locked it. Where is he, my creator? Save me. Save me. His face is outside the window, watching me burn. Watching me burn!' She began to tremble and put her hands to her face now.

There was a cry – I heard a chair topple as gentlemen hastened their ladies from the room. But others, men, came to crowd about the foot of the platform where Maria stood.

Maria straightened her body. 'I came to another place,' she continued. 'They beat me, put me in the streets to sing. I could not speak. I could not speak. I knew no words. Victor had given me no words.'

Now there was a gentleman on the stage, speaking urgently to Wheeler. But Wheeler was in his seat, slumped over, his head in his hands. I stood up, Gabriel Mortimer was at my side and we linked arms and went forward, ready to push our way through the crowd to Maria. With my other hand, as we started off, I grasped Mrs Jacoby's hand and pulled her to her feet. Thus we advanced as Maria spoke on.

'I found out the words, then I could not utter them and had I spoken they would have come from a void, from nothing, for I was nothing. I had no beginning –

only Victor – and some shadows in my mind – shadows – a field and a mother – city streets, a man – dark water, pulling me down.'

On the steps of the stage Mortimer, Mrs Jacoby and I stopped short – as Maria extended her arms in a parody of stage craft. Then she said in her own clear voice, as if aping the voice of reason, 'And there you have it, lords, ladies and gentlemen, I speak now but am nothing. Victor Frankenstein made me and I am nothing. He tried to kill me – and I am nothing. And now I have destroyed him, his family, his work and now his life, for he will die soon.' And she began to laugh, a light, merry sound as if someone had amused her, but going higher, less controllable as Mortimer and I, pulling Mrs Jacoby, forced our way on to the stage. Once there Mrs Jacoby dropped my hand and rushed forward, crying to Wheeler, 'Stop this! Stop whatever you are doing to her!' But he turned to her and said, as though his voice were being dragged from his throat, 'I have done nothing to her. She – what has she done to *me*?'

In the meanwhile I had seized Maria and called to Mrs Jacoby, 'Come on!' and we hustled her through the crowd and away to the double doors at the end of the room, joining the crowds attempting to leave. I glanced about as much as I was able, trying to glimpse Victor's poor parents, but in all that mêlée could not see them. As we tried to struggle out there were those who gazed at Maria in horror and pushed away from her, but a vast crowd was after us, jostling and shouting questions, 'Was it real? Is it true? What happened?'

We got through the doors somehow and just outside then, to one side, was a tall, lean man in black, sane and charitable enough, it appeared, to assist. He very quickly took my arm and gently but firmly led me, Maria and Mrs Jacoby through the next room, then quickly through another door to one side and into an empty corridor. Mortimer had disappeared, pushed away from us in the crowd or deliberately abandoning us, I do not know which. The man led us down the corridor, through another door, into an alley. 'We have lost them for a while. I will get my carriage,' he said. We huddled in the alley in dark and cold until, not long after, he came up with the conveyance.

My only thought was to get away from the place discreetly. We dared not go into the main street in front of the building, where those who had attended the demonstration might be assembled in numbers, some repelled, some indignant, altogether unpredictable in their responses. There were those who might think Maria's claim to have destroyed Victor Frankenstein a confession of murder – and perhaps it was. They might try to lay hands on her for that reason and on Mrs Jacoby and myself as her abetters. Others might attack us from fear or from disgust. The curious would surround us. As we stood waiting, Mrs Jacoby recovered a little and in a calm manner, with admirable sang-froid, asked Maria, 'Were you speaking the truth, Maria, or was what you said all wicked fictions?'

Maria did not reply, for then the carriage arrived and the dark-suited gentleman who had rescued us leaned out, saying, 'Get in quickly, I pray you,' which we did and set off smartly eastwards in a direction evidently prearranged between our rescuer and his coachman. I and Mrs Jacoby sat on either side of Maria, the stranger opposite us. This man, I now saw, was about thirty-five years of age, with a long, handsome, thoughtful face, very pitted with old smallpox marks. His dark hair fell to just below his ears. He had fine dark eyes.

I said to him, 'Thank you, sir, for your help. May I ask where we are going and why you help us in this way?'

'My name is Simeon Shaw. I am vicar of St Michael and All Angels near Spitalfields. If there is any truth in this young woman's tale, it may have much bearing on the subject of the soul.'

Beside me I heard Mrs Jacoby, who was plainly fatigued and whose own conversations with her soul had become less and less frequent during the day, give a weary sigh. 'I think, sir, I should like to go to Russell Square,' she said. She turned to Maria quite naturally and asked, 'Maria – should you like to go home?' She displayed no surprise when Maria said, in a clear and pleasant voice, though tired and indifferent, 'It would be too dangerous. A crowd might assemble and kill me for a witch or a murderess.' I, however, was truly astonished. If Maria had been in a trance, how did she know what she had said?

Mrs Jacoby responded drily. 'I'm glad to find, Maria, that recovering your voice has not altered your nature. You still think first and last of yourself.'

Maria answered, 'Of whom else should I think? You have heard my story now. I have no conscience – I have no soul.'

Simeon Shaw interrupted this extraordinary exchange hastily, 'I came to the demonstration today interested in finding out if the hidden soul of a man could emerge during a mesmeric experience. For, under that influence a man might come closer to God. What I heard, Miss

Clementi, interested me deeply. I am uncertain of the precise nature of what we saw tonight, whether side-show, horror tale, or what, but I feel, bewildered as I am, some kind of mystical truth may have been involved.'

'A devilish truth, if that is what you want,' Mrs Jacoby said sharply. 'I should have thought it your duty as a clergyman to avoid such things, not embrace them. Do you know all you said tonight Maria? Have you any recollection?'

But she did not reply. I felt her body, very limp against mine in the carriage. It was as though she were ill. Often enough, my mind had pictured Maria's body close to mine. Now it was, but in these circumstances I did not know what to think or what I felt. Mrs Jacoby continued.

'Understand now, Maria, that what you said under Mr Wheeler's mesmeric influence was this – that in some manner Victor Frankenstein had created you and another, whom you called Adam – that he had attempted to burn you to death and dispatched the man to some dreadful place far away, hoping, no doubt, that he would die there. And you claimed to be nothing and no one – and rejoiced in Mr Frankenstein's coming death, laughing like a maniac the while. Maria – we must know more.'

To this she made no answer. She did not care about us, I realised, nor about anything that had occurred. It was as if she had dropped to our planet from the moon.

'Maria's tale,' said I, 'tallies all too well with what I was told by Donald Gilmore, who was present as a boy on the Orkneys, the cold and lonely sea-girt place described by Maria.'

And – 'So there is supporting testimony,' murmured

Mr Shaw the clergyman to himself. Though he had rescued us, I began to like the man less, and mistrust him more. He was plainly in the grip of some kind of theological fanaticism concerning the human soul, researches perhaps best left alone and certainly irrelevant to our present predicament.

Meanwhile we rode on. Maria lay back in the carriage, her eyelids flickering like someone in a fit.

'Where are we going, Mr Shaw?' I asked him. 'These ladies are in my charge.'

'To my church,' he said.

'Never,' said I, with more firmness than I felt. 'These ladies need fire and food, not the cold interior of a church. I thank you for rescuing us but I think now we had better make our own arrangements.' I had no idea what these might be. It seemed to me then it would be undesirable to go to Russell Square, equally so to Gray's Inn Road. In either place we might face arrest or hostile crowds. Should we find some quiet suburban inn to pass the night?

Shaw offered another suggestion.

'If you will not come to the church, then let me take you to the house of my Bishop. He will see to your comfort and I will explain things to him.'

Mrs Jacoby asked, as if to herself, 'And what will you explain?'

Meanwhile he had leaned forward and shouted up another address at the driver. The carriage turned into the road and clopped back in the other direction.

'The soul – ' Shaw began.

'I have no soul,' came Maria's dreamy voice.

Shaw said, 'But this is blasphemy. Why do you say that?'

'Mr Frankenstein told me so,' she said, then lapsed into silence again.

'Can it be possible?' questioned Shaw.

'Frankenstein is a villain,' declared Mrs Jacoby. 'I have never heard such blasphemy in my life. You are speaking now, Maria. So speak. For the love of God, tell us everything you know.'

But whether from fatigue, illness or obstinacy, she would say no more.

A few minutes later we evidently reached our destination, the Bishop's house, for we passed through gates, drawing up on a paved semicircle before the house. A servant let us in. Mrs Jacoby, Maria and I were ushered into a small, fireless room where Mrs Jacoby and I took seats on wooden chairs while Maria extended herself on a hard leather sofa, which had seen better days. Shaw went off to explain matters to the Bishop. Some fifteen minutes passed. We grew colder and colder and it became more and more apparent that the Bishop was extending no welcome to Mr Shaw, or our party.

Mrs Jacoby expressed this first: 'The Bishop will have none of us or of Mr Shaw's theories of the soul. He sees danger to the Church, or himself, in all this. An argument rages while we freeze. We need fire and food, perhaps a nurse for Maria.'

'And almost certainly a lawyer,' I agreed. 'What to do? I think we must risk going to Gray's Inn Road and on the way I will leave a note for my lawyer Mr Finborough to attend immediately. We must resolve this matter of Maria's confession.'

'Made under the influence of a mesmerist, and therefore nonsense,' Mrs Jacoby said decidedly. The godly woman of Chatham now pushed firmly from the door, the practical woman in charge. 'Very well, let's go to Gray's Inn Road. We must at least have some shelter. When we arrive, you must descend from the carriage at a distance and scout out the house before we enter. If anyone is encamped there, either outside or inside, you will not return and I and Maria will go elsewhere.'

'Where then?' I asked.

'That will be my business,' said she.

We left without ceremony, finding ourselves in a cold empty street near St Paul's Cathedral with Maria supported between us and no conveyance in sight. A sleeting rain began and I said, 'We had better reconcile ourselves to walking,' which we did. At Mr Finborough's in Fleet Street I left a message asking him urgently to call on me. I persuaded the reluctant servant to hasten to a nearby mews where there were carriages for hire. Meanwhile we waited in a hall, Mrs Jacoby and I standing, Maria on the only chair.

Mrs Jacoby, looking at Maria, said severely, 'She could speak if she would. She feigns illness.'

I admired the pragmatism of her approach but I knew, and so must she, there were grave considerations here. Had Maria's outburst been caused by insanity, had she been put up to the entire thing by Wheeler, or had she said what she did deliberately to mislead and cause sensation? It could not be as simple as that. I knew Gilmore's story; furthermore, Elizabeth Frankenstein was dead, Frankenstein himself was gravely wounded, and there was the missing man-beast I had seen so close to all of us, even now being hunted for attempted murder. It was hard to believe Maria's statements merely insane or deceitful.

It was equally impossible to believe, in a reasonable world, in Victor's conducting deadly experiments with human beings. Yet he had done something, some terror had taken place on Orkney. But what?

Above all, I wondered what of Cordelia? I had earlier that day envisaged myself on my way back to her this very evening, undertaking the first part of my journey home before darkness made it too difficult. Yet here I was in a carriage going back to Gray's Inn Road, worse entangled than ever in this sinister affair.

Mrs Jacoby now addressed the fainting Maria, in no uncertain terms. In fact she grasped her by the shoulders and shook her. 'Speak up, you bad, wicked girl. You could speak – if you would – we know it. Why did you say what you did? What is the truth? Do you understand you must now face the charge that you killed Frankenstein? Certainly you will be suspected of involvement in his attack. And where did you come from and what is your proper name? You must tell us now.' And with this she dealt her a blow across the face.

Maria did not respond in any way, so Mrs Jacoby gave her another buffet. Then Maria, with an access of strength of which she had not seemed capable, wrenched away from her and cried out in an anguished voice, 'Adam!' She leaned past me, over my lap and grasped the handle of the carriage door. Even as I lunged to stop her, she had thrown it open and hurled herself over me and out of the vehicle. Few could have so quickly evaded my too-late clutching hands; even fewer could have jumped past me from the moving carriage – and landed on their feet. But this Maria did.

As Mrs Jacoby shouted for the carriage to stop I leaned from the door, and saw her running ahead down the road, then veering into an alley. I heard her cry, 'Adam! I come to you!' Then she was lost to sight, gone into the darkness like a frightened cat. I suppose we both realised we had little chance of finding her, though we combed the streets in different directions for an hour, I on foot, Mrs Jacoby in the carriage.

When I returned to Gray's Inn Road I was not surprised to find Mrs Jacoby there with two burly men from Mr Wortley's, the magistrate, wishing to question me about the whereabouts of Maria Clementi. Word of what had taken place at the Royal Society had been spread quickly to all ears.

There was little we could tell these men that would satisfy them. To get rid of them I suggested Maria might have gone to Mr Frankenstein's house at Cheyne Walk and for the same reason Mrs Jacoby suggested the house in Russell Square, the theatre and certain other places. But neither of us believed that Maria would go to any of them. She was in pursuit of her Adam, whoever and wherever he was.

The men left and we sat alone for a while, thinking of Maria roaming through the darkness, going towards, I supposed, this Adam she was trying to find. Mrs Jacoby told me she knew nothing of him, adding, in a tired and disillusioned manner, that she had come to London at the demand of her conscience, but only with the gravest doubts, knowing that anything concerning her erstwhile employer could not go healthily or right. This had proved to be the case. She said she was not a young woman, had not slept the previous night from anxiety, had come post-haste from Chatham that morning and, though it was but eight o'clock in the evening, she craved to end a long and disquieting day. She wished to hear no more of the business, or think any longer about it. With my permission she would go upstairs to bed and leave early next morning by the coach to Kent, glad to be out of it all. At least, she said, with a weary smile, she had been plunged back into the hectic and disreputable life she had once led in such a way that she could never again doubt the wisdom of leaving it, even for her present dull and melancholy life. And she added kindly, 'Mr Goodall, you summoned me back for the best of motives, to a life I had renounced out of shame and remorse. I do not complain. But this affair is not over. No – it is not over – it will get its tentacles about you and drag you to the bottom of the sea. And I note what perhaps you have not – there is no disinterested person in this matter other than yourself. Gabriel Mortimer has profited handsomely by Maria's effort since he first discovered her in Ireland and hoped to do better if she could speak. Wheeler put her on show to placate his rich masters and increase his own fame – after this recent horrible display he may have failed but who can tell about that, the world is very strange. And Nottcutt – Nottcutt was a bored degenerate in search of sensation, now, I suspect, trying to distance himself from the affair which has shocked his parents.

'But these men, Mr Goodall, involved themselves in this matter desiring some personal satisfaction. Alone among them, you did not. Let me tell you, nothing concerning Maria Clementi is without criminality, or frenzy, or lust. She is a magnet for men with empty pockets or fevered brains or bodies. She may not be entirely to blame. After what we heard this evening, whatever the real truth, it appears at least that she has been very ill-used.

'But you, Mr Goodall – Jonathan – are innocent. You must withdraw from this matter before it overwhelms you. You have, I know, a worm of curiosity in your brain, a desire to know more, a feeling truths can be discovered which will transform the world. The light of reason, you think, can be induced to play over the world; all will be transformed; we shall live in Paradise.

'Well, my dear, I am older than you and have seen the world transformed twice, once by revolution in France and then by the Emperor Napoleon, and this second transformation widowed me. I have no love for transformers and no desire to see a world transformed again. Leave things as they are, Mr Goodall. Leave them alone. Go down to the country, live with your good young woman and your family, look to your land and care for the families who tend it for you. In short, cultivate your garden, that is the best a man can do. Do not lose your grip on the good and the real, I beg you.'

After Mrs Jacoby had retired to bed I was very thoughtful. She had told me forcibly what I knew, gave me the advice I gave myself. Maria had gone; I did not think she would return. I determined I would visit Victor next day to see how he did (revealing nothing of today's transactions even if he were in a state to understand what was told) and then go swiftly back to Kittering before I lost everything I held dear.

SIXTEEN

Next day, early, Mrs Jacoby and I parted with all good will. I secured a place on a coach leaving for Nottingham at eleven that morning and went to pay a visit to Victor before my departure.

Mrs Frankenstein was greatly distressed when I arrived, and not very welcoming either, for she and Victor's father had seen me getting Maria from the room at the Royal Society and discovered from the men calling at the house that she had escaped. She thought me to be Maria's accomplice. Maria must be found, Victor's mother insisted, and forced to confess the dreadful allegations she had made against Victor were false.

However, the poor woman had greater cares even than that. Victor, she told me, had the day before gone into a high fever: the doctor despaired of him, saying that during the attack vital organs must have been penetrated which were now mortifying. Little could be done, said Victor's unhappy mother, stricken with grief at the approaching death of her son – and deeply bewildered also. Apparently at three the previous morning he had called for pens, paper and ink which his nurse had been afraid to refuse him. Since then he had been propped up in his bed, dreadfully ill, writing furiously. His mother had not discovered all this until daylight broke when she went in to see him. Finding out what he was doing she had pleaded with him to stop. He would not; she dared not force him to do so, even though she knew this exercise could only weaken him further. He was still there, she told me, leaning against his pillows, scribbling, the bed strewn with written-over sheets of paper.

'He cannot be writing an account of his attack,' she said. 'For why would he write so much? He gave me the keys to his desk, also, and insisted I bring certain papers to him. When I refused he became so agitated I was forced to comply. Please,' she urged, 'please, Mr Goodall, will you go to him, try to calm him, persuade him to rest?'

I agreed I would do this and went upstairs to Victor's room.

The situation was exactly as Mrs Frankenstein had described. Victor lay propped up, yellow-faced and indescribably thin. There was a roaring fire, a nurse sitting by it but doing nothing, for there was nothing to do. As I came in she gave me an anxious look, then rose to her feet. Around Victor's head was a bandage, badly stained. I guessed even there his wounds were not healing. As I approached I saw his face was beaded with sweat. In his hand was a pen, spluttering ink as his hand moved rapidly across a tablet of paper propped on a writing desk he had against his slightly raised knees. His position looked painful; his whole face and attitude spoke of agony. The entire expanse of the bed was covered with sheets of paper, some written, others containing diagrams and chemical formulae. As I went to him the nurse intercepted me, saying, in an undertone, 'Can you persuade him to cease this frantic work?'

I nodded and went to the bedside. Victor looked at me and smiled, a mere rictus, yet somehow, his sunken eyes were more peaceful than they had been for many months. I was happy to see it, yet I grieved.

'Jonathan,' he whispered in a rasping voice – he had much trouble breathing and as I came closer I heard his breath sawing in and out – 'Jonathan, I am glad to see you. Will you take my papers?'

'Of course I will, Victor,' I answered.

'There are also some notes of my work.'

I nodded again.

'Do not let my parents see this,' he said, gesturing with the pen at what he had been writing. 'They must never see it.'

'I will make sure of it. But Victor, you must cease writing. It is doing you damage.'

'I know, but I have finished now,' he said. 'Jonathan, there's no help for me. It is over, and I am glad it is. For I have made my world a hell and I can live in it no longer. These papers are my testament and my confession. Preserve them, and preserve the scientific papers also. I have made advances, scientific advances in a way no man should have, but the knowledge, Jonathan, the knowledge –' And as he said these last trailing words it was in the tone of a man who speaks the name of a lover. Then he gasped, 'Gather them up. Hide them. Take them with you when you go.'

I could do no more for him than relieve his mind of anxiety, so I gathered the papers roughly in a bundle and put the weighty document into the inside pocket of my coat. I removed the pen from his hand and the desk from his knees as he shut his eyes, unutterably exhausted.

As I went about my business with the papers and the desk I tried to speak levelly to him, but kept my eyes from him, for they were full of tears. 'Victor,' I said, 'whatever you have done you have repented and repented bitterly. There is a God who will forgive you. May I not send for a clergyman now, to whom you can unburden yourself and who will assure you of that forgiveness?'

He sighed. Each word, as he spoke, gave him pain. 'No churchman could – no priest could give me absolution for what I have done. God himself could not forgive. I have abrogated His rights, done what no man should do – I have tried to make myself a god.'

'Victor,' I groaned, weeping openly now, 'this stern Lutheran conscience – this self-punishment – it cannot be right.' I fell to my knees beside his bed.

'Jonathan,' he said, 'I cannot truly repent unless I destroy my work, the work from which so much evil has come. And that I cannot – no – *will* not, do. Read my pages – read them.'

'I will,' I said. 'Of course I will.'

His eyes closed again, and 'Farewell,' he whispered. His breathing became harsher, more laboured. In his physical struggle he forgot me, then, I saw, lapsed into unconsciousness. So, 'Farewell, Victor,' I said and kissed his brow and left, weeping.

I descended the stairs. At the bottom, Mrs Frankenstein awaited me. I must not show her the papers, the writing of which had cost her son so dear, yet I knew she would think she had a right to them. Reaching the bottom tread, I wiped the tears from my eyes, looked at her anxious face and saw it change as she realised from my expression that I, too, believed her son would die.

I told her Victor had finished writing and had given me his papers to put in order. I would take them to the country to do so. Mercifully she did not ask me then for copies. Her first – her only thought – was for Victor, whom she, bidding me a hasty farewell, went up stairs to tend.

Later I received a letter from Victor's father asking for his son's last testimony. I replied telling him that as he knew his son had been in a high fever when he wrote, the pages, alas, were rambling and incomprehensible, the diagrams and formulae appeared meaningless. I had therefore, I said, taken the liberty of burning the pages, which would have brought no further credit to his name. The work he had done and the feelings of his friends and family for him would remain his best memorial. Mr Frankenstein did not reply to this letter.

It gave me no joy to refuse the request of the bereaved father but I had promised Victor I would keep his papers from his family. And had I broken that promise, what consolation would they have brought? Certainly, possession of the last testament of Victor Frankenstein over the years I have held it, has brought me no peace of mind.

I set off for Gray's Inn Road, where I would pack my small bag and go to the coach, but I had not gone very far on the frosty road, under a laden, yellow sky, when the first snowflakes began to blow in my face. Before I reached home I was walking half-blind through the snowstorm and there was an inch of snow on the ground beneath my feet. I suspected the coach might not set out in such conditions and this proved to be the case. When I arrived with my bag in the City, the coachman was well muffled on his seat atop the vehicle, six coach-horses in their traces. Then he began to clamber down again, passengers put their heads out of the coach windows, demanding to know what was going on. The coachman shouted that reports from further up the road told of snow having started early in the morning, and roads already half-blocked. To proceed would be folly.

I was sorely tempted to hire a horse or a private carriage and blunder my way through to Nottingham. But a moment's consideration made me realise this would have been madness. Cordelia, given any choice, would prefer a delayed husband-to-be to a frozen corpse by the wayside. I returned to Gray's Inn Road, frustrated and melancholy.

It was therefore in Cordelia Downey's little parlour that I sat alone before a roaring fire and, putting the pages of drawings and scientific information aside (and I have not looked at them since), I began to read the account Victor Frankenstein had scrawled that day, from what was to prove his deathbed.

SEVENTEEN

'*I know myself to be a dying man, killed by that beautiful creature I created. I know I am irrevocably doomed for I have committed the unforgivable sin, the ultimate blasphemy. I have usurped my Maker, and made life. I made a new Adam and a new Eve. They are wicked; they have proved my punishment. Oh, my poor wife and my little son, innocent even of the knowledge of what I had done, now both dead, dead as if by my own hand.*

'*But I must be as brief as I can for I have little strength or time left to me. I dread being unable to finish this, my account of my life, of my sins.*

'*The first creature I made as a young man was a brute, though whether I created a brute or turned my creation into one, I cannot say. However, it was that creature which turned against me, which destroyed my life and, made it a waste. He taught me what I had never known before, bitterness, loss of hope, self-contempt.*

'After this occurred I would not learn the lesson it taught me. A wiser man, a less ambitious man would have felt remorse – as I did – then, never meddled again in such business. But I, arrogantly, thought I could put right what I had done – by going further. It came to me that the softening effect on my creature of one of his own kind, but a woman, might render him harmless and thus decrease my guilt. And he wanted one, a bride, as he called it, moaning, 'My bride, get my bride,' in his strangled tongue until I was forced to lock him up to get him away from me or I would have killed him.

'His nature was not all savage. His fits of bestiality would come on him at random, or when he became disturbed about some matter, big or small. Sometimes, God help him, he was pleading and gentle enough, whining, asking questions and demanding little playthings which I would sometimes supply. Seeing that grisly, monstrous figure in his jail-room, playing like a child with a little wooden horse and cart I had given him, knowing I had created this perversion, this freak of nature – I cannot describe to you the rage and self-disgust I felt. Yet I had brought this awful thing into the world and pride, evil pride, forbade me to do what should have been done – destroy it.

'It was pride made me think I could solve the hideous problem I had created by making a woman for my monster. In my arrogance I supposed I could correct my first error by further effort, by making a woman for my man, a Frankenstein's Eve to match that abortion, Frankenstein's Adam.

'Pride, all pride. Fatal pride, which killed my wife and son and now kills me.

'"Make my bride, my bride, my bride." As I lie here that mumbling grating voice still rings in my ears, as if he were in the room with me. And he might be, for he is still at large, the villain, and will outlive his creator. Does he know it? I think he does.

'In the Orkneys, then, with only the backward inhabitants of that poor little fishing village, a people ignorant, degenerate and barbarous as any Mohican or Apache in America, I thought to hide my beast and make for him his beastly bride.

'I got information from the mainland (a man with money can buy anything he desires if he can find one base enough to supply it) that over in France they could obtain for me the body of a young woman, only nineteen years old. They told me she was a country girl who had come to Paris to sing and dance, had been seduced, was with child – had killed herself. To this day I do not know whether it was suicide or murder. Knowing me to be willing to pay, having found the girl, my villainous associates might well have taken matters into their own hands and caused her death themselves. I asked no questions then, desperate to continue my experiments, find some way of controlling the monster I had made – and improve on him. I had made a man, yes, but a maimed and horrid figure of a man. I thought, if I am to create afresh, let my new creation do me credit. So, using a man desperate for gold as my boatman, I sailed to France and came back with the corpse, a beautiful young woman, whole and undamaged. I needed not fashion her, like the last, merely use the technique I had found of giving life to animate her corpse, thus bringing the dead to life again. I did not this time blasphemously create man like God, as I had *done before, but blasphemously mocked Our Lord Jesus Christ, who brought Lazarus back to life. Yet, one might ask, what harm is there in restoring life to one of God's creatures? Is that not only one step further on from what a doctor, bound by sacred oath, must do? That was what I said then to myself.'*

'Ill-luck dogged me. I shall be glad to leave this cruel world. For who could have guessed that seven years after I left Orkney Donald Gilmore, son of the owner of the fishing-boat I used to transport the girl, would be in London, in the very doorway I was entering? That he would recognise me, that he would tell all he knew?'

'There on Orkney I had my brute locked up in his barn, roaring and yelling, while I made his partner (first removing all traces of the child she was to bear). Soon I had, living and breathing, the bride, the wife for my monster. She was so beautiful, soft-haired, smooth-skinned – so beautiful. And, because her mind was wiped clear of all memory, she was so innocent, primally innocent. Even as she awoke from her unconscious state she looked into my eyes – mine was the first face she saw in her new life – and smiled such an innocent smile, the smile of a baby.

'At that moment it came to me, with some vast pang which tore through my body, that I could not give over this angel to that beast. For all I knew then, he would kill her. If he did not he would brutalise her, make her, for all her beauty, as foul as he was. She was mine, I thought. Not his – but mine. Thus, one sin gave birth to another.

'In his barn, knowing my work proceeded, the beast grew more noisy and importunate. I had to send the men in to quieten him, but even then he would not be still. And all the while I contemplated teaching my woman – my blasphemously titled Eve – to speak, to teach her what she must know to be my consort. And yet, within days, even before she understood anything, she yearned to go to where he lay on straw in his barn. At night I was forced to lock the doors, for otherwise she would creep out at night and be found outside the door of the barn at morning, half-frozen and completely ignorant of what she had done. When he cried and called out she would gaze towards where the cries came from, rise and try to escape, to be with him.

'I could not, would not, give her to him.

'Yet, while he, that accursed creature, was there to distract her, I knew she would never be able to love me properly. So, I concluded – I must get rid of my maimed Adam and, when he was gone she, my Eve, would be truly mine. I was employing madman's logic, and like a madman, I did not know it.

'I might have killed him, but the villagers in that primitive place were becoming suspicious. They suspected me of magic – and even Gilmore might have balked at helping me dispose of the corpse at sea. And – in any case – I made him. The creature was mine. Something prevented me from destroying my own creation with my own hands. I had attempted it before many years before. God help me, the result was that he as good as killed me.

'I therefore took him to Dublin, drugged and crated, and released him. Describing him as my manservant,

I accused him of the theft of my watch and had him searched. The watch was on his person, of course, for I had put it there. I handed him, and his future, over to the authorities there, to let them decide whether to hang or imprison him. I scarcely cared which, only to get rid of the creature. He did not understand what he was supposed to have done, nor what was happening, and stood in the dock when he was tried, blubbering mumbling and grimacing.

'When they led him away – the verdict was transportation to Australia for the rest of his life – he held his arms out to me, tears running down his vile face, blubbering, "Master – master." Even as they hauled him, struggling, down the passageways to the place of imprisonment I heard him calling out again and again those fatal words, "Master – my bride, my bride."

'I quit Dublin, thinking soon he would be taken away to live out his life in chains on the other side of the world, and if he did not die there, in that inhospitable land, then certainly he could never more return to Europe. Alas, ugly, feeble-minded, misbegotten as he was, he was strong. He survived that life of cruelty, that fierce climate, the deprivations, the beatings. He survived and somehow contrived to return here, still seeking his bride.

'Even before I returned from Dublin my Eve – Marie had been her name, while she lived – had begun to deteriorate horribly, not in her body, which was beautiful as ever, but in her mind. Once I was gone with the creature she at first wept, then enticed both my guards. When I returned to my house the first sight I saw was the woman with my guards at my table. There was

a bottle of brandy in front of them, my Eve was sitting on the knee of one, bare to the waist, as he fondled her and she laughed. The other guard stood before the seated couple and the woman – my woman – had her head buried in his waist. The men were terrified when they saw me and fled. I took her, my angel, and beat her black and blue. At first she screamed and tried to escape, then began to fight me tigrishly, biting, scratching and kicking. When I had done with the beating I let her go and she went and sat in a corner, her eyes following me – but when I looked at her, when I bent down and tried to reason with her and tell her what she had done was wrong, she would not meet my eyes. When I put my hand upon her she flung it off.

'But the next day she was miraculously changed, an angel, and I praised her. The day after that she was good, and the next. But the following night she ran away. Next morning, from dawn on, we searched and found her on the hillside only two miles off, exhausted, for she had run and run frantically, not knowing where she was going, hither and thither round in circles. Tired as she was, though, she fought to get away from us. She bit my hand to the bone. That taught me she had learned cunning. She had pretended to love me, to be good in order to disarm me and put me off guard so that she could make her escape. Before, she had been licentious and violent in her behaviour – now she was cunning! She had learned guile in the space of a week! And they say man is innately virtuous! Jonathan, he is not. He is bad from his moment of creation. And woman worse – that I know.

'From that point forward she was the most evil

creature in the world — cruel, dishonest, needing continual watching and guarding. She shrank, spat, flinched from me, growled like an animal when I came near her.

'Yet — I loved her! But she hated me, that was the truth of it. She would run vainly to the barn all the time, if she got the chance, to look round its now-empty space and howl. She refused food, would not come to the table, would not wash or be washed, sat on the floor in a corner, glaring at me through her matted hair, that hair I had found so beautiful. The lovely face was smeared. She grew thin. In my despair I became angry. What could I do with her? She was no fit bride for me now. Now she was only fit for that other hideous creature for whom I had created her.

'She was mad. I, too, became mad, prowled the house at night, fell sobbing on my knees to her in the corner where she lay. Where was the beautiful creature I had brought to life? I did not want this filthy, hating, hateful woman, if woman she was. I wanted my beauty, my creation — but she would not return. I wept to her and tried to lay my head on her angry breast. Then I did, alas, it is bitter to confess, what I had never done to any woman before, nor ever thought I would. I took the creature, raped her while she loathed me and I was sickened by her. We lay together on the floor after that awful, bestial act — and she smiled at me — such a smile! Such a devilish smile. Then she became affectionate, as it seemed, clung to me, followed me, would not have me out of her sight — and smiled and smiled — that indescribable smile.

'I could not truly believe she had come to love me for

my brutality. I thought this smiling guise was a deceit, that she feigned love now as once she had feigned obedience, to put me off my guard. And this time, I feared, instead of running away as she had before – this time her plan would be to kill me! For I thought she hated me and knew some part of myself now hated her.

'And all this confusion of mind produced only one clear thought, though it may have been a thought springing from madness. I knew I must kill her or she would murder me. I must finish this dreadful experiment in the creation of life or the restoration of the dead, whatever I had done. I must finish it and quickly end this futility and shame. I had been on that island only six months – a man may wipe out six months of his life, I reasoned, and go back to a normal life. Why, I thought – a man may with any luck wipe out years of degradation, shame and error, may hide all, put all behind him and go back to a contented and reputable life, enjoying the society of his fellows and the love of a wife – all crimes gone, healed, swept away. Many men have done this. Why not I, so I reasoned? Why not I? Why should I suffer the consequences, for the rest of my days, of those short, ill-fated years spent in creation of creatures who betrayed me? Why, said I to myself in my pride, should I be forever doomed for having made scientific advances of the most extraordinary kind (for they were, Jonathan, they were).

What harm would it do if I thrust back into oblivion those creatures I had made? It was not murder. They were not human, either of them. How could they be? The man I made. The woman I had brought back from death, rescued, like some Orpheus rescuing his *bride from the Underworld. I would be doing nothing but what a potter does when he finds his work come from the kiln malformed or spoiled in some way and breaks it.*

'*So I reasoned — so it was done. We packed our goods, a fire was set and matches put to it and the house burned down as the woman lay, drugged, inside. Or — so I thought.*

'*I began to travel in places far from civilisation. I had a need to be alone for a time and my ever-restless mind led me to making a study of the languages of the regions to which I went. Gradually I became calmer, and found some kind of forgetfulness. I lived among the Algonquians of Upper Canada for a time, studying their languages and customs. On a visit to New York I met my beautiful wife, Elizabeth van Dahlen. I believed, truly believed, my penance done, I might leave my solitude and create for myself a new, happier life.*

'*We came to England to live. It was here in this house my child was born, here I continued my studies of language, those studies which brought us together, Jonathan. But how dreadful that those very studies made it possible for me to come close to Maria Clementi and in that way meet the fate which had been awaiting me for so many years.*

'*A week ago was the anniversary of the day I saw her. It was last year, at the end of winter. My wife and I had gone to the opera. You will remember Maria singing* "Remember Me" *that afternoon here at Cheyne Walk, Jonathan? Now, alas, the irony of that, her satire, will become clear to you. For that night she was taking the part of Dido, poor deserted queen, in* Dido and Aeneas.

'At first, like any other individual in the audience I was charmed by her grace and the uncanny beauty of her voice. Her hair was dark, she was made up for the stage – how could I recognise in this talented, fêted, worldly creature that girl who had opened her slate-grey eyes to mine – and smiled – when she was born a second time, reborn at my hand?

'Yet slowly, as the performance continued, a strange sense of familiarity stole in on me – and with it a sick longing to come closer to Maria Clementi. My wife sat beside me in the box. I have never felt further away from her. As the performance continued my yearning grew greater, deeper than I ever felt when about to marry my first wife – whom I loved but almost as sister, for we had grown up together – or when courting my second wife, for, lovely as she was, to me she represented the final lifting of the cloud that had hung over me since Orkney, was the symbol of my re-entering the world of my fellow beings. But these are mere excuses for my feelings for Maria: what I knew was that we were twin souls, locked together, creator and created. I was afraid, of course I was afraid of what I felt for the actress, but my longing was too strong for fear.

'It was when Maria came to the footlights at the front of the stage to acknowledge the rapture of the audience that I knew – I knew! Older by seven years, her hair darkened by artifice, I still recognised her as the woman to whom I had given life on Orkney. I had of course believed her dead in the fire. But I knew now she must have escaped for this was her – my Maria – my Eve – my Maria Clementi.

'I was forced to go home that night with my wife

and pretend that all was well. But all that night I did not sleep and knew that when morning came I must begin my plans to meet her.

'*I showed the caution and cunning of the true villain. Resisting the temptation to rush and find her, I went to the theatre later that day and found Gabriel Mortimer. I told him I was a student of languages presenting him with credentials of every kind. I said I had heard that Miss Clementi was mute (as all London knew) and that it might be possible for me to discover the cause of this condition and, that done, perhaps help her to find her speaking voice again. This was something of a risk, for I saw at once that this "impresario" was as good as an exploiter of the young woman and thought therefore that he could have invented the tale of Maria's dumbness to attract more fame and attention. And if that were so, Maria could expose me for what I was – if she remembered.*

'*I cannot tell you what rage I felt then, and thereafter, when talking to Mortimer. This man was daily close to the woman I loved, knew her in all her most intimate moments, was, my fevered brain told me, perhaps her lover. But I had to suppress this hostility for I needed Mortimer to get me to Maria. I enquired into her past and heard she had been found barefoot, singing in the streets of Dublin, had been taken up by the better people in that city and produced at their entertainments, then brought to London by Mortimer, who added that in spite of her unprotected past she was a good young woman, ever attended by the most respectable of chaperones.*

'*As we conversed I acted with calm and cunning. I took Mortimer in, I think, but he was so hopeful I* detected of restoring Maria's voice, for profit, I believe he would have made a friend of Satan if he had promised Maria the gift of speech. Though I was not sincere, I had no desire to help Maria to speak, for she might denounce me. I only desired her. When I thought she was dead, I thought my desire for her died. It had not. It merely lay frozen ready to thaw – and now was the time of the thawing.

'Mortimer detected none of this. He suggested I visit Maria's companion, Mrs Jacoby, who would say if she thought me acceptable to Maria.

'How I endured the three days before the appointed afternoon I do not know. I writhed, I twisted, was restless, distracted, incapable of any concentration. My mind was filled with suspicion about Mortimer's relations with Maria; and I cursed in advance the old woman who could, if she chose, keep me from her. I was forced to send my patient wife to the Felthams, so that she would not see my trouble and begin to question me in an attempt to share a burden I could not reveal to her. Truth to tell, I wanted Elizabeth from me. She stood between me and my desires. From the moment I saw Maria again, I wanted my wife away. This confession causes me profound shame, but it is the truth.

'Came the day of our meeting. In the small drawing-room at Russell Square with Mrs Jacoby's solid presence guarding the tea-table, I saw again, close to, the face of my Eve – Maria. For it was she. I knew it instantly. She was composed, charmingly but quietly dressed in pale blue. She greeted me with a handshake, a pleasant smile and no apparent recognition in her eyes. Gone was the girl who opened her eyes and smiled her first smile at

me. Gone the filthy, biting, scratching creature that girl
became. But it was her.

'How could I guess that licentious, spiteful creature,
subject to violent, uncontrolled emotions of every kind,
had exchanged her undisguised lusts and malevolence
for a quiet air and smile, like that of a Sicilian who will
wait ten, twenty, thirty years for his revenge? She knew
me, of course. She had known of me for many years, I
have no doubt. But she had not come to me. She had
waited for me to go to her so as to disguise her plans
and make my final torments at her hands more dreadful.

'The lessons designed to help her speak began. To
cover my desires I enticed you, my friend, to share
those periods of instruction with me, and for that I can
only say I am deeply sorry. It was, moreover, useless,
for when she rejected me I became desperate, as you
know very well. It was all the beginning of her making
my life a hell.

'Of course, my relations with my poor wife grew
worse. I did what so many other weak and treacherous men have done, allowed her to grow bewildered,
denied there was aught wrong, became angry when
she piteously asked me, yet again, if anything was the
matter. Intimidated by my anger and vehement denials
she then ceased to ask me anything, kept herself away
from me as much as possible, grew thin and pale. I felt
nothing for her but irritation when she was trying to
make me speak and relief when she withdrew from me.
I felt no guilt, no shame, nothing. I just wished I could
remove her entirely so that I could pursue Maria without
impediment. What a wretch I was – how unconscious
of my own wickedness – and would that I had made

Elizabeth leave my house and return to America. Had I done so, she would be alive now, and my child also. But she was too devoted, too loyal to leave me when she knew all was not well with me, and death was the reward she reaped for that loyalty.

'It terrified me, Jonathan, when you told me of having seen that monstrous Other just after my wife was killed. I truly believed the crime had been committed by a robber disturbed in the course of conducting a theft. When you told me you had seen a man in the garden, even then the horrid suspicion came to me that the creature I had made had somehow found his way back from the other side of the world to punish me and lay waste my life. And all the while Maria beguiled me more and more, turning me into her slave.

'Elizabeth was killed and I – I was so sunk in the mire I was almost happy. I felt so little for her by then, my head was so full of Maria. I thought little, even at that moment, except that now I could court Maria without shame, bring her to the house, marry her.

'Hugo and Lucy saw me let her in just after my wife's death. She held me off, though, until that last night, fatal for me.

'I still did not suspect her. It was Maria, of course, who killed my wife and child, Maria who attacked me. The man, that ogreish creature I had made (and whom I believe she paid to have brought back from Australia) was innocent of anything.

'She waited to tell me until the night came when she acceded to my desire to possess her. She kept me in torment for two weeks after she came to the house,

an agonising two weeks, for she allowed me to kiss
her, allowed me every familiarity other than the final
embrace.

'She came to my room late one night when the
house was dark and quiet and in the bed in which
I now lie dying she gave herself to me, coiled about
me serpent-like, draining me of vital force, consuming
me. I knew I would never have enough of her. She
was Lamia. She was not Eve, my Eve, but Eve's bad
counterpart, Lilith.

'It was as I lay there, weak and extinguished yet utterly
happy, that she pointed to the scar on her shoulder, past
relic of the fire on Orkney from which she had escaped.
She began to whisper. It was at first not so much what
she said than that she spoke at all, which astounded
me. She had been all along capable of speech! And
then, as she leaned over me in the bed, her long hair
trailing, I began to hear what she said – that she had
known me all along, that she had escaped my fire and
smuggled herself aboard a boat to Ireland, been picked
up hungry and cold on the shore by tinkers and taken
to Dublin. It was true, she said, she could not speak at
first, for she had no language. Had she been able to
speak, she would have had nothing to say. She had no
experience of the commonest things of life, no account
of herself to give, no past, no memories except certain
little trailing recollections of France as a child, then a
sharp memory of Paris streets and betrayal. Her only
vivid memories were of Orkney, of me, of Adam, my
creature. Otherwise, she knew nothing, remembered
nothing, so what good would words have been to her,
even if she had them?

'Later, she said; after Mortimer had picked her up and made her fortune, she heard I was in London, for my name at least she knew. When I walked into her net, she said, she played with me a little, then killed my wife and child, to play with me a little more, then made me pant after her like a dog. I lay beneath her, her strong hands pushing me down, her hair half-blinding me. And then, as if all that were not hideous enough, she said, smiling — oh, the horror of it — "Adam is here. I hid him for a long time in your garden." Then she brought her face closer to me and said, "We have met every day in his hiding place. I stole your food for him. Are you not amused? Each day, hour on hour, I have made love to him. Do you laugh? He loves me, Victor Frankenstein, as I do him. We cannot love anyone but each other. And now he and I are here — both here — in this house and you who made us, who treated us as you would and disposed of us as you wished when you found you could not love us — you will die yourself, at our hands."

'And even as I thought in horror of graceful Maria being savaged by that maimed, inarticulate monster, the bedroom door burst open — and he was there. I saw in the doorway the huge body of the man I had created, heard his heavy tread, felt his great hands seize me as a child seizes a doll and looked into his savage, gloating face. I could not cry out. Effortlessly, he pulled me from my bed, threw me over his shoulder and ran downstairs with me. In the drawing-room by the window he held me, my arms pinioned at my sides, my feet barely touching the floor, while she, Maria, in her nightdress, stabbed and slashed at me in a frenzy with a knife saying, "This is for the blows you struck, this is for the hunger you did *not assuage, this is for the cold, for the whip, for the chains."*

'I remember falling, hearing a crash of glass as I suppose the beast sprang out through the window to make his escape. Then I recall Maria bending over me crooning, "Now you die, my dear creator and Adam's creator. Now you die." She must have been found thus as if very grieved at my injuries, by those who came into the room. I knew nothing of this, for I had lost my senses.

'This, Jonathan, is my most dreadful story. I am sorry, my friend, that I deceived you and used you to mask my passion for Maria. I am sorry I deceived you, to protect myself when you began to come across the truth. I could not endure the thought that all would soon know what atrocities I had committed. I could not bear to believe it was impossible to return to Eden, the world before I constructed my downfall. But that garden, once one has eaten the fruit of the tree, cannot be re-entered. I know there is no hope for me in this life; I think there is none in the next. I believe I'm going towards damnation.

'Jonathan, forgive me, and pray for me if you will.

'Finally, for the love of God, protect yourself and your family from these two abominations I have made. They will have fled and I do not think they will be caught. Beware of them, I implore you.

'God bless you, dear fellow. You have been loyal to a fault to your most unworthy friend. If you can, I beg you to pray for me, pray for Victor Frankenstein, little as you may think he merits your prayers.'

EIGHTEEN

M y Lord – I must add a postscript to the dreadful
and pathetic tale of Victor Frankenstein, one of
the unhappiest of men who can ever have walked the
earth, and creator of his own unhappiness. For there is
more. You may perhaps see in Frankenstein's account
the ravings of a man enfevered and near death. Often
and often I have tried to persuade myself that is all there
is to the tale, but, alas, there is too much evidence to
support its substance.

You will recall that I read Frankenstein's final testimony at Gray's Inn Road on the afternoon of the day
he died. I read, as would have anyone, with growing
horror, yet the doubt, that twilight of half-seen shapes
and forms in which I had been living had been almost
as terrible in its way as was the horror, fully revealed.

Yet what frightening intellectual questions it raises!

I took no note of Victor's warnings about the
uncaptured pair. They had no reason to attack me

or mine, if his account were true. *If it were true.* For to believe Victor's account one would have to believe that Victor had made – created – revived from the dead – two seemingly human beings who ought never to have existed.

As in an old tragedy Victor had dared the gods, usurped their power, suffered direly as a result of his own ambition, pride and vanity. Even in his final, desperate confession one can still see traces of that lack of humility. Perhaps to those vices he also added one further sin, that of inhumanity. For though that misbegotten pair were not as we are, one constructed and brought to life, the other brought back from the grave where she should have been left peacefully at rest, were they not in some ways human? Did they not share, in however warped a manner, some of our humanity? The art of Maria Clementi – the passion of the monster for his bride – are those the attributes of mere beasts? Are they not close to our human qualities?

Let us settle that, though not man, they were not beasts. My friend had not treated them as men, for they were not. Yet they were not quite beasts, but he had used them as such; tried to kill them as a man does a dog – worse – as if they were cattle bred and slain for man's use. To me it seemed strange that he had never, from beginning to end, contemplated the way he should treat these creatures or in what relation to him they stood. As for my part in this tragedy – I was no protagonist, more like one of those ancient tragic choruses, deluded and bewildered, admonitory, ever powerless to alter anything.

As I dropped the pages to the floor, wishing them out

of my hands completely, I knew poor Victor would all too soon be standing before his own Maker, to receive final judgment.

I pitied him.

As my story will have demonstrated, my Lord, I had up to that point been an indifferent Christian, no Christian at all. My religion had been a background to my life, but I had thought, as many men do, that it was a matter more for women and children, not the concern of grown men. This view, unacceptable as it might be to the Church is common enough, we all know. But Victor's terrible story compelled me to contemplate many grave matters which had never concerned me before. Principal among these questions was that of redemption. And I knew, even as the last pages of Victor's own history left my hands I must make one final effort to find a way of convincing my poor friend, before his death, of the mercy of God. For he seemed certain his God was about to condemn him to eternal hell. I could not endure that this would be his last thought before he died.

My acquaintance with the clergymen of London was small, but I found Simeon Shaw at the bedside of an old woman of his parish and hauled him out into the snow to go to Cheyne Walk. On the way I confided to him much of Victor's story, which he half-believed. As the coach crawled forward through snow, he made the telling point that if Victor Frankenstein had bequeathed to me his scientific papers I might be in possession of the secret of the creation of life. He then ambitiously suggested I put these papers into the hands of the Church – by which I think he meant, himself.

My lack of faith in religion has always been inextricably mingled with my lack of faith in the clergy, for, throughout the ages, has not the priesthood suppressed knowledge to incease superstitious power among the credulous? Therefore I said plainly and in an angry manner, 'Mr Shaw – I am taking you to the deathbed of my friend in order that you may convince him there is a Redeemer who will forgive all if he truly repents of his sins. That, and no more. I will give you no papers, and if you indicate to anyone that such papers exist I shall deny all knowledge and claim that you are inventing. If you wish to do any more than bring the consolations of religion to a dying man then we will turn the coach round here and now and go back.'

I felt sure of my ground here, having already the impression that he did not stand well with his Bishop, being considered cranky and perhaps in some respects not altogether in his right mind. At all events, this statement silenced him. But his suggestion that Victor's papers might convey the secret of his experiments has haunted me over the years, thus my great relief in handing the documents to you.

We were let in by the butler, very grave. His master's parents were with him; he was dying. I took Simeon Shaw upstairs.

I had no place in the room where parents were bidding the last farewell to their only son, I went downstairs. Poor Victor, I learned, died only a little later. While Victor's mother had held one of his hands, Mr Shaw had the other in his own grip. They said Shaw told him of the all-embracing mercy of God. Victor had squeezed the clergyman's hand, unable to speak, and died. But that is often said on such occasions. Whether Victor was consoled, whether he had truly repented, I know not.

After I blundered down that chill staircase and as those final scenes took place upstairs I remained in the salon where full of melancholy thought. I pressed my forehead against the freezing panes of the long windows. The two guards were there, playing cards, as ever. Then something – some shadow – caught my eye. In the moonlight on the snow-covered lawn, two hundred yards away from me, were two dark shapes dancing, one huge and lumbering, crippled, in a long black flapping coat, the other a graceful, bird-like, swooping figure. They danced in the snow and ice, bowing, capering, gliding, following some pattern understood only by themselves. Even he, ungraceful as he was, showed a peculiar, clumsy agility. They were completely caught up in each other.

I saw Maria – for I knew one of the figures was hers, the other being that of her monstrous bridegroom – raise her arms above her head and twirl into his embrace – then he released her and she spun again on the white carpet of their outdoor ballroom. The dance continued, their feet making black patterns on the snowy grass. I closed my eyes, thinking the sight an hallucination – but, no, when I opened them again, there they still were. Now the courtly dance had become wilder, a twirling, stamping fandango, as they swung each other round by their extended arms. It ended as they went into a long embrace. Then straightaway they parted and still hand-in-hand began to run, as two children will run happily towards some morning

game on a summer's day, away from the house and
into the trees.

I believe that must have been the moment when Victor
died. This was the triumphal dance of the creatures he
had brought into being.

'Two kings – a deuce.' I heard one of the guards
say.

'No – curse this light,' said the other. Then a gust
caught their one candle and it went out. We were left
in the darkened room with only the moonlight coming
through the window. The figures outside had gone now.
There was only the trampled snow they had left behind
and a trail of their footmarks over the grass.

It was, of course, a horror beyond anything. I should
have called out the guards, now cursing as they searched
for their tinder to relight the candle. But what would
have been the point? To find and seize that pair would
have taken a regiment, and I knew that now they had
accomplished the death of Frankenstein, their maker,
and they were reunited, they would go far away.
Frankenstein was dead. They had found each other;
they needed no more.

I left that mournful house without speaking to anyone.

That night Cordelia, bolder than I, came to me over the
icy roads. We were married a month later after the thaw,
when sun and light returned and spring was making its
first efforts to warm and cheer the world. In that year
I gave her Victor's terrible account to read and when I
asked her opinion as to what she thought I should do
with it – should I preserve it, put it into other hands,

burn it? – she advised that Victor's testament along with the drawings and formulae should be safely locked up, where no one could ever find them. And this we did. It is only now, as I am trying to settle my affairs and my conscience (though, I hope still looking forward to many years of health and contentment), that I have felt I must solve the difficulty of what to do with this material.

But, my Lord, there is a further postscript to this affair which I feel I must relate. This event occurred some years after those I have described when I and my wife were on holiday in Switzerland. We were sitting with Flora and our little son at the edge of one of that country's many beautiful lakes, gazing with pleasure across the body of water at the view on the opposite side. Here there was a small, grassy foreshore, behind that a forest of tall pine trees. It was a clear day, the distance between ourselves and the other side of the water being some two hundred yards. Suddenly my wife rose to her feet and cried, 'Look! Jonathan – what is that?' On the verge of the lake opposite us walked two figures, one huge, lame, clumsy, the other, nearer to us, a woman, small and graceful. And between them, holding the hand of either parent, a small child, by her clothing a girl. Then they were gone, into the pines, too quickly for either of us to be perfectly certain of what we had seen, whether they had been there at all. We gazed at each other, though, in some horror. My wife asked me, in awe, 'Was it them, do you think?' But I could not answer her.

My Lord, we may have been mistaken in what we saw but, since you are to be the recipient of Victor Frankenstein's papers, and since they may contain the secret of how to create human life by artificial means, it is vital that you should be told this later part of the story. For – imagine – if those figures were those of Frankenstein's creations, his Adam and his Eve, if the child was a child they had between them, then not only are they still at large but between them have bred a child like themselves. And so might any other creature produced as they were. Will such children, if nurtured as ours are, be different from us, be more or less evil than we are ourselves? Who, what will they be?

And another sober thought came to my mind then. If the child was born of Maria Clementi, then she might be the only surviving child of Victor Frankenstein himself, fathered on the woman he brought back to life, his creation. Dreadful, impossible thoughts, my Lord, but dare we in conscience ignore them?

It is almost twenty years since I saw those figures. From time to time there are still moments when I dread the reappearance of that child, grotesque or inhumanly lovely in form – an angel – or devil? What might she be? I pray, my Lord, I shall never encounter her.

For the rest, I confide these papers to you in the confidence that your good judgment will help you to decide better what to do with them. Whatever you decide may I make one plea – that you offer up a prayer for poor Victor Frankenstein – and another for me, witness to these frightening events. Then also, if I may presume to suggest it, I suggest you pray also for yourself, who now know all the story of Frankenstein, and to whom it is given to decide what to do with his heritage.

I remain, most respectfully, my Lord, your servant,
                                        Jonathan Goodall.

or less